The Fourth Order
A Thriller

Gary Parker

Pretorious Press, Inc., Publisher
Rancho Mirage, CA
© 2018

About the Author

In addition to *The Fourth Order,* Gary Parker is the author of numerous published articles, most recently for Anthem Publications' *Vintage Rock* Magazine. His work has been favorably reviewed by such publications as the *Los Angeles Times* and the *Pittsburgh Post-Gazette.* In addition to *Win or Go Home,* a work of non-fiction published in 2003, Gary is the author of *The Original Jethro Tull, The Years of Glory* (McFarland Publishers, 2018). Gary can be reached via his website *www.garyparkerwriter.com*

Acknowledgments

Sincere thanks are justly directed to the following, without whom...

Sue Conner, Anita Bartholomew, Richard Craig Anderson, Michael Dortch, Laura Taylor, Michael King, Dale Conner, Barbara Kingsolver, Dennis Hayes and Shane Gericke

Kim...

For all you've done,
For all you are,

...This one's for you.

Chapter 1

May 15th 1980

The place is one long funeral song, a porridge of pitched tents and tumbledown shacks, reeking of rotting trash and human waste. The air, radiating the oppressive heat of a Gaza summer, has forced residents from their tents into the open air, in search of whatever shade they can find. Crouched out front, a woman, frail, dark, damaged, lowers her top and hoists a baby to her breast. As the infant takes her nipple, a sound like thunder breaks loose and the low rumble of heavy machinery shakes the ground. A shout spirals up in the heated air.

"Police! Police!"

Sirens fill the sky, wailing in spectral waves. A flash moment later, a security detail consisting of three police cars roars through. As they pass, the tall man, a visitor to the camp, senses an opportunity. Grabbing his young son and daughter by the arm, he dashes after the speeding vehicles.

A minute later, the detail pulls up in front of a crumbling shack where just outside, a fitful, surging mob has gathered. As shrieks of "Let him go!" fill the air, the police muscle their way to the front of the milling throng where a uniformed man with a body like an overstuffed suitcase waves a nightstick at a boy of approximately sixteen. The boy, eyes wide with terror, fends off blows.

The visitor and his two children, gulping air from their two block run, arrive just in time to see a member of the security team edge up behind the young man and smash his skull. As he does, the skin on the back of his head opens and rolls back. After wobbling for a moment, the boy slumps to the ground. As he falls, the others pounce on him, hammering his head, back and legs with their nightsticks. Screaming in pain, the young man pulls himself into a fetal ball to ward off further punishment. Repulsed by the carnage, the crowd ignites, while knots of boys standing a few feet away hurl rocks. Reacting to the threat, police wade into the enraged throng with sticks flying, driving them back. Those that resist are pummeled into submission.

After what seems an eternity, the young man, now starting to convulse, is yanked to his feet and with his arms twisted up behind his back, is dragged to a police car. As they pass, the visitor and his two children get their first good look at the quarry. His head, a grotesque orb, is bloated from the beating he's endured. Blood pouring from his head streams down his face and drains into his right eye. Repelled by the sight, the boy squeezes his eyes tight, while his sister, feeling sick, turns to flee. Reacting, her father yanks her back, forcing her to confront the scene. Watching nearby, a woman, fifty-ish and heavy-browed, confronts the father. "Take them away," she shouts, spittle drops spraying his face. "No child should be forced to witness such evil!" After cursing, then shoving her aside, the visitor tightens his grip on the children and lunges toward the police. As he does, both children tumble to the dirt. "What is his crime?" the visitor screams at the security guard, taking no notice of his prone children. "Tell us! What is his crime?"

Slamming the door to the police car, the taller of the two security officers barks a reply. "He's a terrorist operative," he declares, "plotting against the state."

An old woman with scars like claw-marks on her face shouts a curse. Hate filled cries rise up, then disintegrate at the swing of a nightstick. After bullying their way through the mob, the police storm back to their vehicles and with a hail of sirens, race away. The young children of the visitor, still lying in the dusty street, begin to cry.

The boy is eight, the girl is six. The place is the Qualandia refugee camp in Gaza. The year is 1980.

A half-hour later, the father and his children are perched on a hill overlooking the camp. "You've seen it with your own eyes," he says, gesturing toward the squalor that fans out below. "A proud people, forced to live under the heel of oppression. Thirty years ago, they were evicted from their own lands -- their homes and possessions stolen from them, forced to live like animals."

Kneeling, he fixes his children with a stare. "Were you troubled by what you've just seen? Well, it was nothing. Those people have experienced far worse. Homes torched and gutted and then rebuilt only to be infected with Zionist bullies. I've seen mothers and fathers shot down, their bodies bleeding and ravaged, left in the street to rot for trying to protect their children. "Children," he said, " no different than you!"

Horrified by his words, his daughter cries out and runs for the sheltering embrace of her older brother. In a flash, her father pulls her away. "No," he said, clamping his hand down on top of her head, forcing her eyes to meet his. "Always face the truth, however painful. And never forget what you've seen this day."

At home forty minutes later, the children eye each other apprehensively as their father wedges his shoulder against a bookcase and with a grunt, shoves it aside to reveal a room they have never seen. Once through the door, he guides them down a steep flight of stairs to a dimly-lighted cellar where chairs circle a flaming cauldron. As they descend, the children warily eye a huge flag looming over the room showing a triangle encircled by a half moon.

Instructing them to be seated, their father makes his way to a cabinet at the far side of the room. When he returns, he holds an ornate vial in his right hand. In his left he grips a metal rod with a flattened head. Approaching the cauldron, he sets the vial down reverently, then lifts the lid. After murmuring some words in a guttural tone, he turns and faces the children.

"We will rise," he says with his words stretched out. "And you will be with us."

With his right hand, he dips the iron object into the flaming cauldron. A minute later he withdraws it, then dips the end of the metal object into the vial.

Then with the flattened end of the rod glowing with a fiery heat, he moves toward the children.

Chapter 2

March 2015 – Over Machu Picchu, Peru

The storm ripped and slashed, energy coming at the Cessna from all sides. The plane banked hard to the left, but the more the pilot tried to break free, the more entangled the craft became. When the engine sputtered, then quit, Reid Temple looked at Jason DeMir, who stared back at him with an enigmatic smile. It was then they heard the pilot's voice.

"Hold on Mr. Temple, we're going in."

The impact ripped the plane in two, scattering debris and rupturing the fuel tank. When Jason DeMir came to, his first sensation was of agonizing pain radiating from his left shoulder. Looking down, he saw that the joint had been ripped open, exposing a grisly visage of bone and cartilage.

A scream pierced the air.

"Help me! I can't move!"

The cries were coming from the cockpit. DeMir, gripping his damaged shoulder and grimacing, staggered from his seat. As he did, his boot snagged an exposed electrical wire, sending a spark racing into a pool of gasoline puddled nearby. In an instant, the inside of the plane ignited, sending a sheet of flame racing toward the cockpit and the trapped pilot.

Swiveling his head, DeMir saw that Reid Temple, blood gushing from a head wound, was pinned beneath a row of crushed seats. Audible groans made it clear that he was still alive. With the pilot in immediate danger of burning to death, Jason shinnied down from the wreckage and with lurching steps, made his way to the cockpit. After yanking the door open, he saw that the pilot's legs, contorted and pulsing blood, were trapped beneath the twisted metal of the plane's control panel. The terrified man, eyeing the approaching flames, was frantically wrenching his body left and right in an effort to free himself. Reaching in with his good arm, Jason grabbed hold of him and yanked, only to be driven back by heat and smoke. Coughing, he tried once more, only to be forced back again. At that moment, flames reached the cockpit, triggering anguished cries from the pilot. "Do something!" he implored Jason. "For God's sake, don't let me burn!"

Realizing that the plane must have a fire extinguisher, DeMir scrambled to the passenger cabin to locate it. As he did, he saw that the flames had spread and now threatened Reid Temple. Unable to find the fire extinguisher and with his friend's life hanging in the balance, DeMir dashed toward Reid. After pulling Temple safely from the stricken craft, he raced back to the cockpit where he found the frenzied pilot with his hair now aflame. Again and again, Jason tried to yank him free, only to be driven back by the inferno. As his clothes began to ignite, the pilot's begging grew more anguished. "Don't let me burn Jason! Please! Please don't let me burn!"

Sobbing and desperate, DeMir spun around, scanning the ground for something, *anything* he could use. Then he spotted it: a piece of broken wing strut lying just feet away. Grabbing it, he dashed back to the cockpit and with one vicious, violent blow, ended the man's torment.

"Once more, Mr. Temple, once more."

Standing for the first time in two weeks without crutches, Reid Temple eyed the young man who urged him forward. "Are you a sadist or physical therapist?" he asked flashing a rueful smile.

"No hand rails, Mr. Temple, remember?"

Letting go of the supports beneath each hand, Reid, weaving noticeably, edged forward with halting steps. As he did, he winced.

"Pain?" the therapist asked.

"Nothing I can't handle," Temple replied through locked teeth.

Following the crash, Reid had opted to remain in Peru for treatment of his injuries instead of returning to California. His ailments, which included a collapsed lung and broken leg, had responded well to treatment. His mental state was another matter. The expedition over Machu Picchu had been his idea, leaving him feeling responsible for the pilot's death. Jason DeMir, ensheathed in a cast that extended from shoulder to wrist, had done his best to cheer Reid up in the days following the crash. No one, Jason reminded him, least of all the pilot, was oblivious to the inherent danger of dodging a Peruvian thunderstorm in a Cessna the size of a backyard tool shed. After all, it could've been any one of them. He was right and Reid knew it. But long days would pass before his spirits started to lift.

For all its tedium, being laid up did have its advantages. Sure, the rehab was tough and he'd limp for the remainder of his life, but that was okay. Because when you've had a brush with death, you weigh what's been given against what's taken away. And he'd been given *time*. Time not only to reflect on the crash, but also to think about what he wanted to do with the rest of his life.

For as long as he could remember, Reid had harbored a burning desire to cut through the haze of daily living and do something big. Fresh out of college, he and two friends pooled their resources and started a small software company. At first, the place ran on a shoestring as they toiled long hours, chasing success. Then two years in, a software application designed by Reid to streamline business processes changed everything. Enthusiastically embraced by Wall Street firms, the resulting financial bonanza left all three rolling in money and Reid with enough wealth to buy out his partners. Over the next few years, the company, re-christened Temple Computing Solutions, turned out consumer electronics and leading-edge software that met with huge sales and the company being named by *Fortune Magazine* as one of America's most admired firms.

With money no longer a concern, Reid, forever in search of a new horizon, decided in 2015 to put work aside and pursue other interests. First on his list was exploring the impact of climate change on South America, a cause he'd come to embrace in a region that he loved.

Certainly, being dragged from a burning fuselage by his friend Jason wasn't part of the plan. Jason, who'd been bartending in Peru after backpacking through South America, had become a fast friend despite the decade difference in their ages.

As his body healed, Reid realized he was homesick, not just for California, but also for his first love: technology. For the past several weeks, he'd spent his idle moments mulling over ideas for a new computer operating system. One robust enough to meet modern demands, but also secure enough to withstand the scourge of computer hacking that had plagued businesses worldwide. He had no illusion it would be easy. In an industry where technology changed with quicksilver speed, his OS would have to be cutting edge and so technically advanced, no competitor could match its performance. Never one to shy away from a challenge, he was determined to try, even if he wasn't yet sure how he would bring his dream to life.

Days passed as he weighed options, then one by one, discarded them as unworkable. Then one day in late spring, the clouds parted. He was propped up on his crutches in a dusty Peruvian tavern sipping Pisco brandy when the idea hit him. He'd create an operating system using *molecular nano-technology,* a paradigm that manipulated atoms and molecules to produce lightning fast applications. If he succeeded, the end result would be performance never before seen by the computing world.

Over the next few days, he labored over his laptop, working until every obstacle was confronted and resolved. After a week, he was certain: it could be done. Now, with his vision for a new computing paradigm stiletto-sharp in his mind, he itched to return home to start the hard work that would bring his dream to life. Then, he would share it with an amazed world.

Two weeks later

Littleton Barry 's Gulfstream 550, glistening brightly in the Peruvian sunlight, circled the Cusco airport twice before finally touching down. Barry, celebrated in the United States and Great Britain for his business acumen and philanthropic efforts, was listed by *Forbes Magazine* as the world's third richest man. Having learned of Reid's travails in South America, Barry called to offer the use of his private plane to return his friend to California, an offer that Reid gratefully accepted. The friendship, which began as a business partnership three years earlier, deepened as Reid realized that he and Barry dreamt the same dreams. They were now so close, Barry was among the first people that Reid had called to share his idea for a new operating system. "Funny you should mention that," Littleton replied, "I'm working on something that might interest you."

"Something big?"

"So big," Barry replied, "you'll doubt your own senses."

On the flight home, Reid listened intently as Littleton, who was 50ish and lean, with a well-trimmed Van Dyke beard and a crown of grey curls atop his head, outlined his plan. He, like Reid, was concerned about climate change. If something weren't done to arrest it, he said, the outlook was catastrophic, not just for America, but the entire world. It was clear, he said, that the industrialized countries of the world had to turn away from fossil fuels. But to what? Solar or wind weren't the solution; it wasn't possible, given current technological limitations, for those methods to meet the world's surging energy needs. Maybe nuclear power? Hearing that, Reid shook his head vigorously. No way, he said. Look at Fukushima. The disaster in Japan made it clear that nuclear power wasn't the answer. On this, Reid was adamant. Barry waited until Reid finished then flashed a knowing smile. Reid was right he said. *Traditional nuclear* power wasn't the answer. But what if someone, using a revolutionary approach, found a way to make nuclear energy 100% safe? An approach that promised cheap unlimited energy, but without the risks of traditional nuclear technology. Wouldn't that be a game changer?

His enthusiasm building, Barry scooted forward in his seat, eyes shining with the light of possibility. For the past three years, he said, he'd funded an effort by a team of world-class nuclear physicists to develop a safe form of nuclear energy. At first, things hadn't gone well. But just weeks ago, he said, there was a breakthrough that was breathtaking in scope. It relied on a combustible energy source utilizing graphite pebbles. Pebbles that once passed through a revolutionary processing scheme, would be gas-cooled and unbreakable. Because the pebbles were rupture-resistant, nuclear reactors utilizing the new technology could dispense with the redundant safety systems that plagued nuclear power plants and triggered the failures at Fukushima, Three Mile Island and Chernobyl.

"Bottom line?" Barry said, a world-beating smile on his face. "100% safe nuclear energy."

Stunned, Reid stared back at Littleton.

"Dear God, why that means----"

"Right, " Barry replied, jumping in, "It means goodbye to fossil fuels, goodbye to wind and solar, goodbye to climate change and most critically, hello to a new epoch of human history." After stopping for a minute to let his words sink in, he continued.

"Reid, when I heard about your plan for new operating system, I knew I needed you on this project. Think of it," he said, "a revolutionary approach to energy production, powered by the first operating system utilizing nano-technology." Dropping a hand on Reid's shoulder, he pressed on. "Preserving our environment is a great cause in your life. Maybe *the* great cause. Join me in this quest. Working together, we'll alter the arc of history."

Reid stared out the window as if trying to visualize some distant, visible object. The technical breakthrough Barry spoke of was thrilling. But a project of this scope and complexity, no matter how important the cause, would consume his life for years. It meant everything -- his business, his personal life and probably every waking minute -- would be sacrificed only to pursue a goal, that despite Barry's assurances, might never be reached. Then after a long silent minute, he reached out and seized his friend's hand.

"Ok," he said, "I'm in."

Chapter 3

January 2017

So this is Hollywood, the young woman in the midnight blue convertible thought to herself as she waited out a red light at the wide cross of Highland and Sunset. The postcards in the drugstore racks back home sure hadn't prepared her for this. In the distance, a curtain of yellow haze capped the skyline, forming a gritty cupola that choked the summer sun. "The Los Angeles creed," she muttered to herself with a rueful laugh. "Never trust any air you can't see."

Arching her back, she stretched deeply. The six-hour drive from Phoenix had been hot and tiring and fatigue was creeping up on her like a rising tide. She desperately wanted to soak in a hot tub, but there was no time for that now. They were waiting.

When the signal flashed to green, she hit the gas pedal and after dodging a pair of jaywalkers, rounded the corner. As she raced up Sunset Boulevard, she stared in disbelief at the size and number of the billboards that cluttered the skyline. Sandwiched between advertisements for an Indian Casino and a weight loss program, was the largest billboard she'd ever seen, with an enormous portrait of a blue-eyed blonde squarely at its center. Just below, emblazoned in huge block letters, were the words:

Maddy Daniel

Your New LA News Source

Weeknights at 6 on GBS

She craned her neck and stared at the image as she drove past. Then she erupted in laughter. Well, they *did* say that they were going to make her the biggest thing in LA news.

Up ahead, set against the cardboard brown of the Hollywood Hills, the rectangular lines of the sprawling GBS studio came into view. A minute later, she swung her car into the employee lot and after identifying herself at the guard shack, snagged a parking space just steps from the lobby. After a quick check of her makeup, she grabbed her briefcase and eased herself out of the car. Then, after a deep breath, she dashed toward the GBS lobby, the light swift tap of her high heels sounding on the pavement as she ran.

Once inside, she was greeted by a receptionist. "How lucky you are," the woman said pointing Maddy to the station manager's office, "to get this wonderful position."

Smiling at her words, Maddy said nothing. Anchoring the news in a major media market had always been her dream. Now it was a reality. But lucky? If only. She may have been blessed with looks, but that's pretty much where her good fortune had ended. Marrying at sixteen to escape a dysfunctional home life was just the first in a series of looming humiliations. When her husband, shiftless by nature, decided to stop working, she was forced to sling hash to support them. Shedding him while at the same time attaining a modicum of self-worth had helped her forge a new path that included returning to school. But after receiving her degree in journalism, luck was again in short supply. After months of pounding the pavement and fighting depression, she finally landed an on-air job doing occasional human-interest stories at a small GBS affiliate in Tucson. At first she was grateful for the opportunity, but as time passed, she grew frustrated at being assigned 'soft' news stories instead of more meaty assignments. It took a roiling scandal in Tucson over political graft to finally prove herself. Against the direct orders of the station manager, she pursued the sordid story in her spare time, finally landing an interview with a local real estate developer who directly linked illegal kickbacks to prominent local politicians. The story exploded, resulting in the indictment of the mayor and half the city counsel and landing Maddy on the front page of the Tucson Times. Instead of being impressed, her boss, enraged by her insubordination, threatened to fire her. But when the story was picked up by the GBS network news, things changed. Impressed with her hard-charging work ethic, the brass in New York ordered the station manager to elevate her to the weekend anchor chair. Once there however, her struggles only continued when she bumped up against another obstacle: the 'glass ceiling' of TV news. Women co-anchors were fine, the thinking went, as long as they knew their place. No field reporting, no chasing leads, no scoops. Just sit behind the anchor desk, read the Teleprompter and look good. From the start, Maddy would have none of it. She relentlessly pursued leads, led her camera crews to breaking stories and landed interviews with newsmakers that left her colleagues shaking their heads in wonder or in some cases, envy. Cracking the male-dominated world of TV news may not have endeared her to her superiors, but she had little time to worry about that. She was a journalist, not a potted plant who just read Teleprompters.

Recognizing a star on the rise, the network transferred her to their affiliate in Phoenix, where she was installed as the anchor of the 6 p.m. newscast. After a year, the network, fearful of losing her to a competitor, bowed to Maddy's request and promoted her to Los Angeles. So here she was, her dream of anchoring the news in the country's second largest media market, finally a reality. But did luck have anything to do with it? Hardly.

When she reached the station manager's office, she was greeted by a raw-boned man in his early 50's with a hard-bitten face and bulging cheeks.

"Ed Snider," he said, extending his hand.

"Maddy Daniel. I 'm very excited to be here, Mr. Snider."

Before they went any further, Snider suggested that he show Maddy around. For the next twenty minutes, she was given a tour of the station's studios and video facilities, introduced to co-workers and given an extensive walk-through of the GBS newsroom. He pointed at a room at the far corner of the newsroom where her office was located.

When the tour was done, Snider suggested they stop at station commissary for coffee. As they sipped their beverages, Maddy, barely containing her excitement over her new position, peppered Snider with questions about newsroom procedures and deadlines. To virtually every query she posed, the taciturn Snider either merely nodded or answered succinctly. When they'd finished their coffee,

Maddy, anxious to get settled, got to her feet and extended her hand. "Mr. Snider, I just want to tell you once again how thrilled I am to be here."

After exhaling deeply, Snider took out a LifeSaver and crushed it between his teeth. "Let's get something straight," he said. "You were forced on me by the hotshots in New York who overruled me on my choice. Ok, you were lucky. Maybe it'll work out. But know this: if it doesn't, your luck will run out and you'll be back in Arizona so fast, it'll make your head spin."

Flashing a half-smile, she stared back at Snider. There was that word again. 'Luck.' He'd used it twice. But there was something Ed Snider didn't know. Maddy Daniel was the sole curator of her own success. In the eternity that had passed since she'd struck out on her own, every challenge she'd faced was archived in her mind. But instead of being weakened, every obstacle she'd confronted had only left her stronger. Getting to Los Angeles was a dream realized. And if Ed Snider, or anyone else, thought they were capable of shattering that dream, they'd better think again.

Chapter 4

The call from Littleton Barry in late 2011 had shocked Sahn Rameer. He was working on something that might interest him, Barry said. Could they meet for lunch? Rameer, who never took midday meals, said ok. After all, it wasn't every day that the world's third richest man rang his office.

Pondering the reason for the call, Rameer was sure of just one thing. It better not involve a time commitment. Sales at Rameer Electronics were robust and stock was at an all-time high. Most exciting were the steady advances he and his team had made in the area of nuclear fission, advances that promised great things for the firm's future. In short, he was too busy to think of taking on something else.

Over salads the following afternoon, Littleton Barry laid it out. An idea so grand, so presumptuous, that Rameer had laughed.

"It can't be done. At least not yet," Sahn replied. "Technologically, economically, politically, it's impossible."

Forget the economics and politics, Barry told him. He'd handle those. He then brought up Rameer's research, work that had consumed him for the better part of the past five years. Weren't the reports in scientific journals true? Hadn't Rameer and his team made steady breakthroughs in the area of nuclear fission? Sure, Sahn replied, advances had been made, but safe nuclear energy was still a pipe dream. Rameer Electronics, he explained, was working hard at generating a nuclear fuel source that was 100% safe. But doing so required the creation of a rupture resistant *nuclear pebble* that fueled the reactors, a critical component of the next evolutionary leap in the safety of nuclear power. And it was a goal, that until now, eluded him. At best, a breakthrough was years, perhaps a decade away.

"Do it quicker," Barry said.

"What?"

"I'll support your effort completely," he said. "Drop anything unrelated to your nuclear work, assemble a team of the best nuclear experts in the world and go to work on it 24/7. I'll fund the effort 100% with no limit on capital expenditures. And get it done in three years."

Startled by the audacity of Barry's words, Sahn eyed the ceiling tiles. He knew an undertaking of such scale would dramatically alter the future of Rameer Electronics, halting research and development and undoubtedly delaying work on its new product line.

Sensing the reason for his hesitance, Barry persisted. Whatever financial issues his company would face in pursuit of such a goal, he would cover. He had the desire, the connections and the power to make things happen.

"You see, I have a vision," Barry said.

Sahn eyed Barry deeply. "What is your vision?"

"To remake the motor of the world," Littleton replied. "A permanent solution to global climate change, fueled by a new energy paradigm developed by you and powered by the most sophisticated computing available. A new energy source to usher in the next chapter of human evolution."

Recognizing the grandeur of the goal, Rameer was tempted. Still, he had doubts. "There's no guarantee," he told Barry, "that I can succeed."

"I'm not asking for a guarantee. Just that you try."

"Starting when?"

"Immediately."

Thrown by the offer, Sahn thanked him for the lunch and asked for a week to think things over. As he turned to leave, Littleton Barry said something that made the hair on his neck stand up.

"Mr. Rameer, show the world you've come to terms with your past."

Twenty-fours hours later, a phone rang in Barry's office. "Okay," Sahn told him. "You've got me."

Over the ensuing weeks, Rameer worked steadily to prepare for the challenges confronting him and his team. Key business decisions impacting his computer hardware company were delegated to others as a constant series of prolonged meetings with Barry and his staff gobbled up his time. It was during one of these meetings that he and Littleton encountered pushback from members of Barry's own organization, who, with their eyes fixed on the company's bottom line, viewed the entire effort as insane. Tensions came to a boil in February when Rameer was grilled in front of a room full of board members. To Sahn, the entire episode smacked of a cross-examination.

"You're relying on a nuclear technology known as pebble bed?"

the man, a company vice-president with a voice like rusted shrapnel asked, staring at Rameer.

Rameer nodded.

The inquisitor smirked. "I've done a bit of research on the topic and I've got two words for you," he said dismissively. "Germany, 1986."

"You're referring to---."

"I'm referring to a nuclear disaster at the AVR reactor at Julich, Germany. Plants relying on pebble bed technology –the very same technology you're using – failed and spewed radiation throughout the countryside." As this point, the man's tone turned mocking. "Pebble bed technology," he said, a slanted smile marking his face. "Little nuclear balls that burst, dumping radiation everywhere." Turning toward Littleton Barry, he flipped his palms upward. "And you, Mr. Barry," he said, "want to risk the future of this organization on that?"

With a look of implacable serenity, Barry turned to Rameer. "Sahn, please respond." As seconds ticked by, Rameer sat silently. Finally, after clearing his throat, he spoke. "I cannot dispute what you've said. The technology failed in Germany. It was a catastrophe, a complete disaster."

His inquisitor stared back at him with a look of incredulity. "Then why in hell----"

Rameer cut him off. "I've heard you. Now you listen to me. Yes, the incident in Germany was a disaster. But it cannot happen to our project. *Cannot!* Why? Because the pebbles in the German plant ruptured. Ours won't. Now, let me explain." For the next ten minutes, Rameer, displaying a technical know-how that left his listeners sitting mutely, listed chapter and verse every mistake the German team had made in their deployment, then point-by-point, explained why it wouldn't happen here. When he was done, the board members, if still wary of the plan, were at a minimum, robbed of their momentum.

Littleton Barry rose to his feet. "Members of the board," he said, his eyes shifting from chair to chair. "I believe that Mr. Rameer has made a most convincing case. I move that we vote on my proposal."

Someone at the end of the table spoke up. Mr. Rameer, he allowed, had made a very strong case. However, given the company's responsibility to its shareholders, shouldn't they impose a time limit to ensure that they didn't end up losing their shirts?

Barry nodded. "I've given Mr. Rameer three years. If they don't succeed in that time, all funding will be permanently cut off." Murmurs of assent around the table made it clear that was acceptable. With that, a vote was taken and the project green-lighted.

In March 2012, Sahn and his team, using a development plan that had been subjected to a rigorous series of risk assessments as their template, began work. From the start, their goal was a carbide sphere resilient enough to withstand 3600 degrees Fahrenheit, an intense heat common to nuclear reactors. Anything less and the entire endeavor would be doomed.

For the first year, success hovered out of reach. Then, in the fall of 2014, a series of trials brought them tantalizingly close to their goal when they devised a pebble that easily withstood 3100 degrees. It was the day before Thanksgiving, when, with excitement cresting, the team gathered in the lab to test the pebble at higher temperatures. Standing in a half-circle, the team watched as a lab engineer dropped a pebble into a cylinder that mimicked the inside of a nuclear reactor and applied heat. When the temperature reached 3200, then 3300 hundred degrees, a palpable sense of hope took hold in the room. When the temperature climbed to 3400 degrees and the pebble remained intact, exultant shouts began to fill the air, only to be choked off when it exploded at 3500 degrees. In an instant, a funereal gloom gripped the team.

"It's hopeless," a technician said, convinced they were chasing a dead dream. "We've been at it for over two years. It's imposs--."

Rameer cut him off. "That's enough," he said, nourishing a holdout hope, however small and distant. "We will succeed."

After sending his team home for the day, Rameer returned to his office and eyed his calendar. It was November 2014. For 32 months, they'd chased a dream, only to have it elude them. Now, with just months to go before funding for the project would be withdrawn, it was time to up the ante. A half hour later, he was in front of Littleton Barry, making his case.

"I need help," he told Barry. "For the project to succeed, I need another world-class nuclear engineer."

"Who?"

"Farid Arsham."

Barry said nothing for a long minute, then shook his head. "Find someone else," he said.

Sahn asked why.

"That business in Pakistan a few years ago," Barry replied. "Wasn't he was accused of funneling nuclear secrets to India?"

"Accused, yes," Rameer replied. "But he was later cleared."

"Why this guy?"

"Brilliance, pure and simple. His knowledge of nuclear physics is second to none. In short, he's the best. We've worked together in the past. Anyway, I can't meet this deadline without him."

"Where is he now?"

"In Pakistan doing defense work for the government."

"You absolutely need him?"

"Yes."

A thoughtful silence followed. "Ok," Barry said finally. "he's yours."

Farid Arsham joined a month later. The presence of Arsham, who was whippet-thin with eyes so squinty you were never sure if they were closed or open, immediately boosted the spirits of the disheartened group. From his first day on the job, his task was clear: improve on the bonding techniques that had doomed their efforts to this point.

In late February of 2015, Arsham burst into Rameer's office. 'You'll want to see this," he said, signaling for Sahn to follow him

Making their way to the lab, Rameer signaled for the development team to gather around. After dropping orbs of silicon and pyrolytic carbon into the test cylinder, a technician, his hand looming over a valve, eyed Rameer anxiously, waiting for instructions to increase the heat.

"Take it up to 3400," Sahn said.

As a tense silence settled over the room, the technician applied heat to the graphite spheres. Bit by bit, the temperature was raised until the meter read 3400. Inside the chamber, the spheres held fast. Without taking his eyes off the cylinder, Sahn spoke. "Take it to 3500," he ordered. Gradually, the technician raised the heat in the tube to 3500 degrees. As he did, the spheres, starting to strobe with a fiery heat, remained intact.

After eyeing Arsham for a long moment. Rameer turned to the technician. He then uttered the words that they'd waited nearly three years to hear. "Okay, he said, his voice a conspiratorial whisper, "take it to 3600."

With a trembling hand, the assistant slowly inched up the heat. A moment later, the temperature in the cylinder reached 3600 degrees. When someone in the group tossed up a celebratory shout. Rameer called for silence, "Let's be sure." Eyeing the technician who had started to reduce the heat, he said "No, leave it there."

Seconds eased by with the ticking of a wall clock as the room's only sound. After a minute, Rameer signaled for the technician to end the experiment, then threw his arms into the air, triggering an emotional celebration. They'd done it!

The sound of champagne corks popping in the background, Rameer dialed Littleton Barry. They'd succeeded, he told him. Just short of their deadline, they'd done it.

Upon hearing the news, Barry shouted triumphantly, then congratulated Rameer on his success. Just before the two rang off, Rameer remembered something he'd always meant to ask his partner.

"Littleton," he said, "now that our project is a reality, don't you think it should have a name?"

"It does," Barry replied. "Metrius. We'll call it Metrius."

Chapter 5

"So big you'll doubt your own senses."

Those words, uttered with such conviction by Littleton Barry, were seared into Reid Temple's memory.

Words that now haunted him.

Because now, just short of two years later, Reid Temple was sure of just one thing: he *never* should have gotten mixed up in this thing.

The trouble started a few weeks ago with a knock on his office door.

"Reid, we need to talk." It was Ray Trask, his cyber security guru. Trask was 50ish, with a wire-brush mustache and skin so arctic white that a network of blue veins was visible beneath the surface.

It had been a brutal week. Could it wait?

"No."

Reid looked up. There was something different in Trask's voice, something he couldn't dope out.

"What's up?"

"It's the prototype."

A vein flickered in Reid's neck.

"Not here," Trask said, after Reid motioned him to a chair. "In the lab."

As they left the office, Trask was walking in a funny way he had, listing forward from the waist, as if his upper body was in a hurry to get to someplace his lower anatomy had no interest in going. A minute later, they reached the lab. Inside, the hum of servers filled the air. Settling down in front of his workstation, Trask flashed through folders and files, the clicking of his keyboard echoing the rapid movement of his fingers.

"Here," he said after a few seconds. "Check this out."

On his screen, he'd placed two windows side-by-side.

Reid asked what he was looking at.

"A portion of the Metrius software," Trask replied. "The window on the left shows our help application. The other window shows a version that came from our partners last week."

Staring at the bottom of the screen, Reid quickly realized something wasn't right.

"Wait a second," he said, "their version of our help app is--

"Right," Trask replied. "Twenty megs larger."

Reid eyed Trask with an uncomprehending stare. "Our help app is proprietary," he said. "No one can touch it but us."

"Well, somebody has," Trask said, turning back to his keyboard. There was something else he wanted Reid to see.

"Okay" he said after a few keystrokes. "Look at this."

Eyeing his monitor, Temple saw that he'd positioned two images side-by-side on his screen. He was showing him two identical images from their help app. Why?

"They're not identical," Trask said. He opened a file on his desktop. Look, he said, easing back on his mouse until his cursor was hovering over a cluster of lines.

"This is the code for the prototype image," he said. "See?"

"What?"

He pointed to the lower third of the screen. Down here, Trask said. In the least significant bits.

Was he talking about that code fragment? He was.

"What is it," Reid asked.

"I don't know."

Reid recoiled. "What?"

"I don't know what it is," Trask replied. "Something that shouldn't be there."

Reid, sat for a moment letting his words sink in. "That explains why their directory is larger," he said finally. "Someone's added something to our help app."

How had Trask found it? Dumb luck, he replied with a shrug. Then how did it get by their security programs?

"This thing, whatever it is, is encrypted in a way I've never seen before," Trask said, the tone in his voice toggling between bafflement and awe. "Our software's never seen anything like it."

"How did it get there?" Reid asked. "What was the point of entry?"

Trask sat for a moment, then mouthed words that chilled Reid to his core.

"I think we've been targeted." he said.

"You mean sabotage?"

Trask nodded. "Think about it," he said. "How many people would like to see us fail?"

Reid shook his head ruefully. "Where do I start?" he said. "We're developing a technology that promises to choke off the world's reliance on fossil fuels. Despite our attempts to keep our work secret, it's possible the word's leaked out. If so, any number of folks might be pissed off --- a petroleum exporting nation, a coal producer, an oil company, a deranged hacker, who knows?"

Trask nodded. "And twenty megs of malware slipped into a computer program has the potential to destroy everything we've worked for."

Reid exhaled heavily. Did Trask know what this thing did?

"Not yet," he said.

Dammit, Reid said, his frustration building. He was a world class crypto, the best in the business. He could get rid of it, right? Trask didn't know. This was different. Something he'd never seen before. Besides, finding it was one thing, Trask said, cracking it another. Before he did anything he needed to check out the rest of the product. Reid asked why.

"Because this thing –whatever it is -- is reproducing itself."

His words ignited a white-hot poker in Reid's gut. "What?"

"Yeah, it's spreading from the help app and infecting the rest of the Metrius software."

In an instant, fearful thoughts flooded Reid's mind. Of lives thrown off course. Of career-destroying investigations by US and European nuclear regulatory agencies. Of an international scandal that could bring down three governments.

Jumping to his feet, Reid started to pace the floor. "We've got to fix this," he said, spitting words over his shoulder. "Otherwise, we'll be ruined."

A long silent minute ticked by as Reid worked over what he'd learned. Finally he stopped his pacing and turned to face his colleague.

"Okay, do what you can to get rid of this thing. See if you can isolate it before it spreads any further."

"I'll get my guys on it first thing--"

"No," Reid snapped, cutting him off. "Just you. This can't get out. Not a single word to anyone and that includes friends or family. Is that clear?"

"Okay." Then a darkening came over Trask's face. There was something else, he said. About the software Reid wanted to know? Trask wasn't sure.

"There's been some weird stuff happening recently," Trask said. "I'm worried …." Then with the words teetering on his lips, he stopped.

"What?"

Skip it, he said. He'd been so wrapped up in this project, he was probably imagining things.

"We'll not skip it. Tell me what's bothering you,"

Trask looked embarrassed. "I can't put my finger on it," he said, his voice a hush, "but did you ever had the feeling that something wasn't right?"

"About work or something else?"

"Both." Trask laughed self-consciously. "I know it sounds crazy, I get these weird feelings sometimes when I haven't been sleeping well." He shrugged. "Maybe I'm working too hard. I've just---"

"We've all been working too hard," Reid replied, interrupting him. "Still, don't discount your uneasiness. And if anything unusual happens, let me know. In the meantime, get going on this software problem first thing tomorrow. And keep me updated."

As Reid made his way back to his office, fear launched its' full, frontal assault. Who was doing this to him? A competitor? His success had always riled them…what they had to toil at, he had in his genes. Perhaps a rogue nation or terrorist cell? Someone with a trunk full of warped ideology, hellbent on keeping the world running backwards? Reaching his desk, he grabbed his briefcase and left his office, answers falling away with every step.

Outside, the air had that caramel glow that settles in just after an early winter sunset. A few yards ahead Reid spotted Trask, who'd left by a side door and was just reaching his car. He watched as he climbed in, then heard the rev of his engine as he backed out of his parking space. Then Reid saw something strange. Under an arc light at a far corner of the deserted parking area, he saw an oddly colored tan and black sedan – a car he'd seen somewhere before -- leave its spot, and with its headlamps off, follow Trask from the parking lot.

Chapter 6

In mid-February, an early spring broke over Los Angeles, sweeping aside the cobwebs of winter and ushering in warm days marked by blue skies and cumulus clouds that hung over the city like wind-whipped archways. In the east and midwest, snow still lay deep and heavy, but across southern California, people were lured outdoors from the confines of their homes and offices, happy victims of a conspiracy forged by balmy days and crimson sunsets.

For Maddy Daniel, the arrival of the glorious weather stood in stark contrast to the challenges of her new job. In the past, a steely and unshakable determination to succeed had helped her surmount every obstacle in her path. But her grit was proving to be no match for the sullen and abrasive Ed Snider. Shortly after she'd arrived, he'd flooded her mailbox with biting criticisms of everything from the quality of her work to her physical appearance. Skirmishes with Snider over her image were particularly galling. From the moment she'd arrived, he'd turned a cadre of image-mavens upon on her, determined to convert her into the heavily made-up, blow-dried visage that he believed viewers responded to. Protests that as a journalist, she had no interest in superficiality went unheeded and the flashy image that stared back at her from studio monitors left Maddy sometimes wondering who she was becoming.

But it was dispute over her duties as a news anchor that triggered their most heated clash. It happened in mid-March, when Maddy, who was investigating a tip from a senate congressional aide about possible political corruption in Sacramento, was returning to the GBS studios with a camera crew. As she made her way into the building, she was surprised to find Ed Snider, arms crossed and in a defiant stance, perched outside her office. After motioning her inside, he followed her in and slammed the door.

"Where the hell have you been?" he demanded, a fiery glow in his eyes.

"I've been interviewing a congressional aide about corruption," Maddy replied evenly. "It's a big story Ed, there's kickbacks and---"

"Now you listen to me," Snider raged, cutting her off. "My anchors do not --repeat do not --do field reporting unless I specifically tell them to! Your job --unless I tell you differently --is to sit in front of that camera, read the teleprompter and look good to Joe Sixpack who's at home with his feet up."

"Dammit Ed," Maddy shot back, "I'm a reporter. I'm here to cover the news, not just report it."

"Tell you what," Snider said, jabbing a finger in her face. "You pull out your contract and show me where it gives you explicit permission to do your own field reporting."

"I was under the impression--"

"You were wrong," Snider snapped, stepping on her words. "Any field reporting you do must explicitly be assigned by me. What does that mean? It means unless I specifically direct you to a story, you stay on the set and out of the field and that's an order!" Turning on his heel, Snider stormed out, slamming her office door in his wake.

The confrontation infuriated Maddy, but no less troubling was her relationship with two of her co-workers, Pete Martin and Ashley Stevens. Martin, her co-anchor and a Los Angeles institution, was a large, square-faced man in his mid-50's with a stentorian air and a luxurious mane of dark, grey-laced hair. Stevens, brunette and in her early-twenties, was a former Miss America with no journalism experience that Ed Snider, at Martin's urging, had hired to handle the station's weather reporting a year earlier. Determined to fit in, Maddy turned a deaf ear to station scuttlebutt that Martin and Stevens were involved in a relationship and that he and Snider had lobbied New York to elevate Stevens into the co-anchor position now held by Maddy. Harder to ignore was Martin's constant presence in Snider's office and Stevens' treatment of Maddy that bordered on rudeness. The most troubling moment came in late April, when arriving late to a production meeting, Maddy heard Stevens ask the gathered group in a mocking voice "So where's Los Angeles' number one news source?"

One of the few bright spots was Mako McCallum, an GBS stage manager. At first, Maddy wasn't sure what to make of the young Hawaiian, primarily due to a disconcerting bumper sticker pasted on the back of her car that read "No one ever raped a .38." Maddy soon learned that the genial young woman had been sexually assaulted years earlier and while her anxiety over the attack had diminished, the bumper sticker --along with regular visits to a local gun range—helped keep her calm in the churning metropolis of Los Angeles.

A constant and reassuring presence in the studio during Maddy's newscasts, Mako was a rake-thin, 27 year-old brunette with medium length black hair, a sonorous laugh and a look of perpetual amusement on her face. No-nonsense on the studio floor, Mako was all-nonsense off it and quickly reduced Maddy to hysterics during their first meeting with an explanation of her unique ethnic background.

"Well, the ol' man, he's Irish," she said, launching into a heavy, spot-on brogue; then, switching into a whispery, Hilo Hattie-like cant she completed the sentence. "And my mama, she from the islands." As Maddy collapsed in laughter, Mako continued, a look of mock anger spreading over her face. "Look, it's really not funny. I had a very schizophrenic childhood. I mean, I could never figure out if I was supposed to be step dancing or surfing."

Maddy had never met anyone who could make her laugh more than Mako. In no time, the two women became fast friends, often winding down with post-work cocktails, though Maddy regularly refused Mako's invitation to join her for target practice at the local gun range.

Late at night, before weariness pulled her to bed, Maddy would sometimes make her way outside to the front of the rented house in the Hollywood hills that GBS had found for her. There, leaning against the porch swing, her hair blowing in the evening breeze, she would reflect on the changes in her life. Professionally, she felt conflicted; her climb had been dizzying and friends and family were thrilled with her success. But it all seemed so precarious, subject to the whims of a surly boss and a resentful co-anchor.

It was during these moments that she felt her most alone in the city that she called her new home. To Maddy, Los Angeles was much like the set from which she delivered the news: a glimmering diamond when viewed from afar, but nothing more than plywood and cheap twinkling lights when seen up close. Sometimes her thoughts shifted to the man she'd left behind in Arizona three years earlier. Initially charming and attentive, he'd grown sullen and shiftless once they were married, Dedicated to making the union work, Maddy suggested counseling. When he objected, she went alone. Finally, after a year of enduring neurotic behavior that ranged from silent treatments to outright abuse, she filed for divorce.

Shortly before the winter holidays, a GBS news producer had set her up on a blind date with a political friend, a state senator with offices in Sacramento. That relationship made it to a third date before Maddy, realizing that anything, including watching paint dry, would be more interesting than another discussion on gerrymandering, broke it off.

The real winner was the investment banker who'd approached her one night when she was out with Mako. Whether it was attributable to the amount of wine she'd consumed or the general hilarity of a night out with her raucous friend, Maddy accepted his invitation to dinner. The following night, she found herself in the company of the neediest person she'd ever known, who between bites of his meal, would reach over and pull her into a bear hug. Not thrilled at being viewed as the human equivalent of a beer cozy, Maddy terminated the relationship and was left with a lingering thought she could not completely shake. Were all men jerks?

And so it was during her initial months in Los Angeles that the shadings of Maddy Daniel's professional and personal life assumed a depressing hue. That is of course, until the day she met Reid Temple.

Chapter 7

He moved through the hotel corridor with an unhurried assurance, oblivious to the startled expressions of people who recognized the precisely sculpted face and the shock of straight black hair. As he approached the lobby, Reid Temple noticed a group of maybe fifty people bunched in front of a television, listening with rapt attention to a news report.

"The announcement yesterday of a new energy source has stunned the world," he heard the news anchor say as he pushed his way through the crowd. "Today, developers of this new energy paradigm -- titans of finance and technology -- are fanning out across two continents to share their discovery with the world. Within the hour, two members of the development team are meeting the press in Los Angeles, while in London, a third member is presenting his findings to an elite gathering of climate change scientists."

Once outside, he scurried down a flight of steps, passing two men in business suits who were huddled over a newspaper. "When's the last time you saw a headline this big?' he overheard the man holding the paper say to the other, jabbing it with his finger.

"What's it about?" the second man asked.

"According to this, these three hotshots think they've found the answer to the world's energy problems. And get this… they're practically giving it away!"

"Yeah, right," the second man replied dryly. "That usually means watch your wallet." As the words left his lips, the two broke into scornful laughter.

After he'd walked for five minutes, the convention center came into view, its windows forming a bright band of color and light below the building's double-pitched roof. Spotting him as he approached, a gaggle of reporters gathered outside began to stir excitedly and shout his name. After nodding in their direction, he hurried past the mob and entered the building. Once inside, a production assistant guided him to a waiting room where he could prepare himself before meeting with the press.

Seated inside, a sheaf of notes in his lap, Reid's mind flashed back to the plane flight from Peru with Littleton Barry and his dream for changing the world, a dream that could only be realized with his help.

Now, two years later, it had all come to this. Today, with the world watching and a solemn obligation to his partners, he would stand before the global press and confidently tell them what they'd achieved. But beneath that brazen exterior would be a man tormented by anguished days and sleepless nights. Because now, he and Ray Trask were battling furiously to unlock the secret to a virulent computer virus that was reproducing uncontrollably inside the Metrius software and threatened to destroy everything they'd labored for.

His thoughts were broken when Jason DeMir entered the room. Rising from his chair, Reid embraced him warmly. Jason, who following recovery from his injuries, had accepted an offer to join Temple Computing Solutions in a mid-level position, was soon introduced to Littleton Barry and the two immediately clicked. With Reid's blessing, Jason left his position to serve as Barry's personal assistant. With Barry's schedule growing more hectic and mindful of Jason's abilities, Littleton quickly awarded him more responsibility until currently, he viewed the young man as indispensable.

Checking his watch, Reid asked Jason if his boss had arrived yet. His flight was delayed, Jason replied. He might not make it on time.

DeMir, noticing the dark hollows under Reid's eyes, asked if he was okay. "I'm fine," Reid replied. "Has Sahn arrived in London yet?"

"Just heard from him. He flew into Heathrow this morning. He's meeting the European press in a little less than an hour from now."

Minutes later, Reid was standing center stage before a packed auditorium as cameras flashed, bathing the room in a kinetic light. Above him loomed an enormous banner emblazoned with the word "METRIUS."

After quieting the restive crowd, Reid addressed the throng in vibrant tones. A recent United Nations Report on Climate Change had made it clear, he told them. It said with virtual 100% certainty that discharge of greenhouse gases into our atmosphere was dramatically altering the climate. And if not abated, peoples of the world would soon witness a chain of events that will prove catastrophic to the human race, These included mass extinctions, melting of polar ice caps and a rising of sea levels by more than three feet within fifty years, endangering many of the world's great cities.

"Yesterday," he said, "Littleton Barry, Sahn Rameer and I announced Metrius, a technology that will revolutionize life for virtually every human on our planet. Needless to say, a claim of that magnitude prompted a good many questions, a healthy ration of skepticism and, frankly, some outright derision."

With a sweep of his arm, Reid gestured toward the banner looming over the stage, triggering a renewed burst of flash bulbs. "So exactly what is Metrius?" he asked. "Just this: a scientific breakthrough in nuclear technology that for the first time in human history, will deliver unlimited amounts of energy to all nations of the world safely and affordably and do it in a way…" At this point, Reid paused for dramatic effect, "that not just mitigates the impact of global climate change on our planet, but within five years, guarantees to reverse it!"

A gasp of disbelief broke from the crowd, followed by chorus of excited chatter. After signaling for quiet, Reid started again. "What we're introducing here today is the holy grail for everyone concerned with the health of our planet and our species - a total and permanent solution to global climate change." Extending his arms, he continued. Think what this means, he told the gathering. Goodbye to fossil fuels, oil spills and cap and trade. And most critically, goodbye to the billions of dollars being spent on what was seen as an intractable human problem.

For the next thirty minutes he provided the packed room with details of how improvements to a previously tried and discarded nuclear paradigm called pebble bed enabled them to provide 100% nuclear energy to the world.

"What does this mean?" he said. "Just this: no more Fukushima's," he told the audience. "We---." Then, his voice faltering, he stopped a moment before continuing. "We….we guarantee the safety of our technology," he said finally.

After stopping for a sip of water, he explained that Metrius was an entirely philanthropic endeavor envisioned by Littleton Barry and all proceeds from the project would be funneled to the Metrius Endowment, the projects' charitable arm whose goal was to reduce hunger and provide medical care to underdeveloped nations.

"And here's the exciting part," he told the gathering. "This press conference comprises far more than just a formal introduction to our technology. For today, I'm announcing that nuclear regulatory agencies in the United States have granted us permission to convert the Indian Point nuclear power reactor at Poughkeepsie, New York to a Metrius-compliant implementation by June of this year! And that's not all. For today, I'm also announcing that the governments of Britain and France have also granted us approval to make a nuclear reactor in each those countries Metrius-compliant by the same date. That's right…we go on-line in all three countries in just three months! Once those plants are operational, the goal is to make all nuclear plants in each of those countries, Metrius-compliant within five short years!" The crowd, clearly dazzled by the audacity of the plan, erupted in applause and shouts of approval.

When he finished speaking, Reid made his way to an area cordoned off for the press where he would interviewed by anchors from the major TV networks. Standing off to one side and growing irritated was Maddy Daniel, A few days earlier, despite warnings from Ed Snider that she remain behind her desk, she'd scheduled a personal interview with Temple, only to have him cancel at the last moment. After complaining to his public relations officer, she was promised priority access to him as soon as today's press conference concluded. Instead, she watched with growing annoyance as he spent nearly an hour making his way from reporter to reporter while she waited with her cameraman and sound engineer in tow.

When Temple finally approached, she extended her hand.

"Maddy Daniel from GBS news."

"Very happy to---"

At that moment, Jason DeMir scurried to Reid's side.

"Reid, I'm sorry to interrupt, but we've got to leave. Littleton just landed and wants to see us right away."

"Can't it wait?"

"No, he's leaving on another trip first thing in the morning."

Reid, a look of helplessness marking his face, turned to Maddy.

"I've very sorry, Ms. Daniel. I have to go."

Maddy, saying nothing, nodded grimly. Then turning to her crew said "Ok guys, pack it up. Nothing to see here."

Chapter 8

Ray Trask is alone, thoughts skimming through his head like polished rocks on water. Outside, the craggy California landscape of Riley Canyon flits by his speeding car, but he takes no notice. Every minute of the past five weeks -- the torment of trying to defeat the insidious virus that has infected the Metrius software -- is flashing through his mind.

A 'world class crypto.' That's the label they'd hung on him. And it wasn't bullshit. His reputation may have been big, but his talent was bigger. For over twenty years, he'd taken on every challenge the tech world could throw at him and turned it to his favor. Technology was his life, his muse, his ticket. Nothing he did, didn't work. But now something was broken. Something he couldn't piece back together. Symmetric, asymmetric, stream ciphers, CTR. Anything that would get him to the underlying code. But nothing worked. Because sometimes stuff happens that isn't in the script. Like signals bent back onto themselves, links altered. Energy reshaped into something impenetrable and unrecognizable. Some alien behavior, eerie and illogical, kicked to life by twisted algorithms and crypto streams. Eternal solutions, retracted.

There was no key.

That's what had thrown him. Every encrypted chunk of computer code had to have a key. Kerchhoff established that decades ago for chrissakes. But nothing had worked and now, after weeks of frustration and with deadlines looming, he'd begun to doubt himself. Stabbing thoughts that everything, Metrius, his career, all of it, was about to go up in a sheet of flame. Finally, in a last ditch effort at solving the mystery, he tried something else. Forget the key, find a way to defeat the cryptography. He'd worked through the night, gulping coffee and fighting panic, when at 2:00 am, something shifted in his mind. Something that made sense. The virus was retrieving system data, then using a cryptographic hash of that data as the decryption key. It was brilliant and obscure. So obscure he'd almost missed it: the direct link from the evil minds trying to sabotage the Metrius software to a *mysterious cryptographer from the 15th century who claimed he could conjure the dead*! But now he had it. After weeks of grinding days and sleepless nights, he had it.

In the distance, the morning sun was just peaking the horizon. He should've have called first, he knew that. But he hadn't. He'd be up by now anyway. He'd never known a person who needed less sleep. Anyway, this was news he had to deliver in person. With what was at stake, a phone call was too risky.

With his mind on what he would say when he got there, he almost didn't notice the flash in his rear view mirror. When he looked up, he froze. Just feet from his bumper was the same oddly painted vehicle he'd seen so often over the past few weeks. The one he'd almost convinced himself wasn't following him.

With his heart racing, he glanced around to get his bearings. He was in the remotest corner of Riley Canyon, a mile or two from the summit and at least fifteen minutes away from town and help. He shot a glance at the mirror. The trailing vehicle was following at a steady pace, making no move to overtake him. From where he sat, he could make out the shape of a bull-necked man in wrap-around sunglasses behind the wheel, his face a featureless blur. For the next five minutes, the two cars continued their steady climb up the steep grade of Riley Canyon, the second car maintaining a steady pace, perhaps fifty yards from his.

A minute later, just as he was approaching the summit, he heard the roar of an engine. Looking up, he saw the tailing car accelerating rapidly, closing the distance between them. A moment later, he felt a jarring impact as the car crashed full speed into his. The collision filled the canyon with the grinding clatter of metal on metal. For a flash moment, he radiated shock and confusion. Gathering his wits, he yanked out his cell phone and punched in 911. At that moment, the car jerked forward, slamming into him again. The impact sent his cell phone spiraling from his hand. His engine coughed. His stricken vehicle sputtered and shook, finally quitting altogether at the road's edge. He peered out over his hood, then felt a sinking feeling. Ahead of him was nothing but thin air. His car had stopped just feet from a looming precipice.

He heard the sound of meshing gears, then felt the bruising impact as his attacker smashed his car violently against his, then held fast. The bastard was trying to force him over the cliff! Slamming on his brakes, he brought both cars to a shuddering stop. The roar of the straining engine assailed his ears. Stomping furiously on the gas pedal, he twisted the ignition key and held it fast. "Start damn it, start!" he screamed. A moment later, his nostrils were assaulted by the smell of gasoline. He'd flooded his engine! Slamming the gas pedal to the floor, he furiously turned the key, a desperate attempt to drain his carburetor of excess fuel. The tailing car kept up its ferocious assault. The two cars, spitting gravel and rock, warred to a standstill.

Moments later, the pressure on his car yielded as the tailing car backed off. He saw that his assailant had eased back thirty yards or so, where, with engine idling, he sat watching him. It made no sense. What was he doing? Trask, not waiting to find out, reached for his cell phone and began furiously keying in information. As he did, his attacker quickly brought his car to a full rev, popped it into gear and raced toward him at full speed. Blood pounding in his ears, Trask felt the impact of the car as it powered into his, then the weightless sensation of flying as he was driven over the precipice and into the vast space beyond.

Chapter 9

Five days later, Maddy was skimming through the hundreds of emails that regularly glutted her mailbox when she spotted it. Probably the fourth or fifth one this week signed only by someone calling himself "Constant Viewer." Each message was the same: *"Terrorists will attack this country very soon. I need your help to stop them."*

Because she regularly received similar baseless emails, Maddy was deleting the message when her phone rang. When she heard the voice on the other end, her ears perked up.

"Ms. Daniel, it's Reid Temple." He'd just returned from Europe and had belatedly learned that his staff had promised her an exclusive interview. After apologizing, he asked if they could they re-schedule the following afternoon at his company headquarters.

Still miffed over the previous cancellations, Maddy was nonetheless impressed that he'd made the effort. "Okay," she told him. "See you tomorrow."

A heavy rain was falling over Los Angeles when Maddy and her crew arrived at Temple Computing Solutions the next day. After announcing herself to the receptionist, Maddy and her colleagues were escorted to a pressroom on the second floor. As her crew readied their equipment, Maddy hastily reviewed her notes. Minutes later, Reid Temple, followed by two aides, entered the room. As he approached to greet her, Maddy, taking note of his drawn appearance, wondered if he was ill.

With her sound man indicating he was not yet ready, Temple sat down opposite Maddy and again apologized for the mixup at the press conference.

"Actually, I wasn't completely at fault," Reid said. "My representative was confused by another request from your station."

"Another request? From whom?"

"Someone named Ashley Stevens."

Maddy was stunned. Stevens, the weather girl who'd recently been promoted to a features spot on her broadcast, was pursuing Temple for an interview? She couldn't believe it. The notion that a features reporter would attempt such a brazen stunt shocked her. Besides, this was *her* story.

"I took care of it," Reid continued. "My office called her back and told her I'd be talking to you."

Shaking off her irritation at Ashley's actions, Maddy said that she'd heard gossip related to Metrius.

Temple asked what she was referring to.

"Rumors that the project is being delayed."

Temple shifted uneasily. "No," he said after a long moment had passed. "Everything's fine. We'll be on-line this June."

At that moment, Maddy's sound man flashed a thumbs-up, indicating he was ready. After being queued by her cameraman, Maddy began the interview.

"Mr. Temple," she said, "Metrius promises a revolution in----"

At that moment, an aide to Temple rushed into the room, a look of urgency marking his face. After apologizing to Maddy, he knelt and whispered something in Temple's ear.

Nodding, Reid got to his feet. "I'm sorry," he told Maddy, "but I need to take this call." Struggling to quell her frustration at this latest interruption, Maddy signaled to her crew, then watched as Temple hurried from the room.

When Reid returned a few minutes later, she was stunned by the change in his demeanor. Completely transformed from the pleasant individual of just minutes earlier, the man that now stood before her was robbed of all strength and vitality. When he opened his mouth to speak, no sound came out at first and he strained to clear his throat. When he finally found his voice, his words tumbled forth in a detached, eerie monotone that made the hair on Maddy's arms stand up. "Something's come up. I have to leave."

Maddy asked if everything was all right.

"I just have to leave," Reid replied. "I'm sorry."

"You can't send me back to the station with nothing."

"I'll make it up to you." He reached for her hand, gave it a quick shake and then, in the same dead tone of voice, said good-bye.

Following his departure, Maddy, her mind on the quicksilver change in Reid's behavior, sat silently as her crew began to pack up. When they were ready, she got up to leave.

Outside, the sky was a cold damp void that peppered the already slick city streets with more rain. Yanking the collar of her coat closer to her throat, Maddy paused in the doorway for a moment to open her umbrella, and then slowly began to make her way back to her car. And with each step she took, she huddled and hunched herself against a feeling she couldn't escape - an eerie and disquieting realization that something was terribly wrong in the life of Reid Temple. And she was determined to find out what it was.

Chapter 10

The crudeness of the man's words fell on the room like a blast of cold air.

"Are you crazy?" he sputtered, his face crimson and distorted. "The entire plant had to be sealed in cement to prevent radioactive dust from killing millions. And now you want to try it again?"

Sahn Rameer, standing before a group of Nobel Laureates and prominent scientists was at the Exhibition Center in central London. As the man continued to berate him, he listened silently, his face registering no emotion.

He'd heard it all before. From representatives of nuclear regulatory agencies, environmental groups and legislative bodies in Britain, France and the United States. On each occasion, precisely and methodically, he explained how things would be different this time. That Metrius, at it core, was completely unlike any energy source ever developed.

What about Fukushima someone asked. Can't happen, he told the gathering and then, with dazzling precision, explained why. "The bottom line? 100% safe nuclear energy."

By the time he was done, his critics had been silenced and scowls had been turned into nodding heads. So he'd do it again tonight. And by the time he was through, even the red-faced man who'd insulted him displayed a grudging satisfaction.

In truth, today's forum was more of a professional courtesy than an appeal for approval. He and his partners had long-since secured the combined license agreements they required to transform plants in the US, Britain and France into Metrius-compliant implementations, Still, Sahn found it satisfying to confront skeptics and watch their as their resistance melted in the face of his data.

After shaking a few hands, he bid everyone goodbye, then made his way outside to London's west end. Because it was raining, he decided against the five-block walk back to his hotel and instead hailed a cab. He'd just opened the door when he heard a voice.

"Sahn!"

Spinning around, his face registered shock as he came face-to-face with a casually dressed man in his late 30's with stringy boot-black hair. It was Farid Arsham, a man he hadn't seen since the Metrius development work ended two years earlier.

"Farid, what are you doing---"

"Nice to see you too," Arsham said quickly, staring back at Sahn through squinty eyes. "May I share your cab?" Then, without waiting for a reply, he firmly grasped Rameer's arm and half-pushed him into the taxi.

"Where to?" the cab driver asked.

"We're celebrating the renewal of our relationship," Farid replied. "Take us to the city's best pub."

Shaking off the shock of seeing his colleague in London, Rameer spoke up. "No, I have a better idea." He turned to his companion.

"I've got a bottle of single-malt Scottish whiskey in my room that I've been saving for a special occasion. Driver take us to the Savoy."

Twenty minutes later, the two men were seated in a lavish suite sipping on their drinks, while outside, heavy rain pelted the window.

"What are you doing in London?" Rameer asked.

"This and that," Farid replied evenly. "So another forum?"

"Yeah," Rameer replied. "Hopefully the last for awhile. As you know, time's growing short. We go on-line in June."

"Speaking of time, let's stop wasting ours, shall we? I'm on to you."

Rameer, saying nothing, eyed his companion evenly.

"Acts of betrayal bear bitter fruit, my friend," Farid said.

"Betrayal?" Rameer said.

"Yes. Of the people who believed in you. Those who've worked for you. And the people you've vowed to help."

Rameer began to slowly shake his head. "I have no idea what you're talking about."

"More games? Must we? Listen, I'm talking about the Metrius sabotage."

"How many know?"

"Just me. For now."

"Why haven't you reported it?"

Farid shrugged. "I'm not sure. Perhaps a misguided sense of loyalty. Or memories of when we stood shoulder-to-shoulder, fighting for the same things."

"Sentiment is overrated."

"But results aren't."

"What's that supposed to mean?"

"I'm thinking of what will happen to you when the word gets out. It won't be pretty." Leaning forward, Farid fixed Rameer with a heavy stare. "You doubt things you were once sure of. I've done the same thing. But I implore you Sahn. Stop this foolishness. Pledge anew to pursue the goal we both shared. Stand with us as you once did."

Rameer, seemingly deep in thought, said nothing. Then noticing that his companion's glass was empty, he took it to the wet bar and refilled it.

"Would you really expose me?" Rameer asked.

"If I have to," he answered, "There's too much at stake."

"If I reconsider, would that make things right?"

"If you're sincere, yes," Farid answered, slugging the scotch back.

"No one else knows?"

Farid, who began to shake his head violently as if to clear his eyes, said nothing.

"I asked you if anyone else knows."

"Mmfllao?" Farid responded, continuing to shake his head back and forth.

"Would you repeat that"

"Mfllfaaoooo…" A moment later, the powerful narcotic in his drink fully hit his brain. Slack-jawed. he looked at Rameer through hooded lids.

"You bast…." Before he could get the words out, his chin dropped to his chest.

Rameer rose to his feet and stared down at the slumped figure with undisguised contempt. "You never could handle your liquor," he said seizing him by the collar. "Here, let me help you up." With a violent motion, he yanked the unconscious figure from the chair and threw him downward, a violent cracking sound piercing the silence of the room as his nose shattered against the tile floor.

Chapter 11

In the days that followed her aborted interview with Reid Temple, Maddy had another skirmish with Ed Snider that roiled the waters of their already troubled relationship. It happened in early April, at the conclusion of her newscast.

"Did you think you could get away with it?" he said, cornering her in a hallway as she left the studio.

Maddy asked what he was referring to.

"Your attempt to interview Reid Temple."

"Who told---.

"That's none of your business," Snider replied. To Maddy, it didn't matter. She knew that her crew, with whom she was developing a close relationship, weren't to blame. She was convinced it was Ashley Stevens.

Maddy eyed Snider evenly. "This is a huge story Ed," she replied, in as measured a tone as she could muster. "Maybe the biggest since the moon landing in '69. It's critical that I cover it."

Snider scoffed. "No," he said, with his voice rising. "It's critical that you follow my orders. Until I tell you differently, you're a news reader, not a reporter."

Seething, Maddy said nothing.

"This goes on your record," Snider said sharply. "One more incident like this and you'll find yourself on probation. From there, your next stop is Tucson!"

When the dressing-down ended, Maddy stood in place, pulling in deep breaths to calm herself. When she returned to her office, she found a voicemail from Reid Temple. Would she please return his call?

In no mood to deal with Temple and his shenanigans, Maddy gathered up her things and started to exit her office. As she did, her phone rang again. It was Reid Temple calling back. Expecting to hear more empty apologies and a promise for yet another interview, Maddy nonetheless decided to answer.

When the call ended, she sat perched on the edge of her desk, completely surprised by what she'd heard. While he did apologize for again disappointing her, he wasn't calling to reschedule their interview. He had to see her, he said. It was important. Would she agree to meet with him the following Sunday at his beach house in Ridge Landing? If so, he promised her a big news story. Unsure of how to respond, she initially hesitated, but the urgency in his voice was unmistakable. She agreed.

On Sunday morning, Maddy hit the freeway and pointed her car southwest towards the beach. The traffic was predictably awful, but by the time she reached the outskirts of Santa Ana, snaking congestion gradually gave way to open highway. Following Reid's directions, she exited the freeway and turned right onto Riley Canyon Road. "The road is steep and dangerous, so be careful,"

Reid had warned her. He hadn't exaggerated. Maddy found the canyon to be forlorn and treacherous, marked by hard darkness and a twisting road that wound from sea level to twenty five hundred feet before finally bottoming out again just short of the coastline.

After exiting the canyon, Maddy swung left onto a dirt road until a dwelling came into view. Making her way down a steep driveway, she brought her car to a stop in front of a shingle-topped, wood and brick bungalow bordered by a skin of overgrown grass on one side and open beach dotted with ice plant on the other. After exiting her car, Maddy stretched deeply.

A voice rang out to her right. Turning, Maddy saw Reid, dressed in a silk shirt and grey trousers, standing on a wooden deck that overlooked the driveway. Dropping to the sand, he approached Maddy and took hold of her hand, holding it slightly longer than she expected. Maddy noticed that he appeared even more drawn than when she last saw him, as if he hadn't slept in days.

Once inside, he guided her to a deck that faced the ocean, where a waiter was preparing a table for brunch. "Let's eat first," Reid said, motioning her to a chair, "then we can talk." The meal, eggs benedict and fruit, was delicious, but Maddy noticed that Reid had stopped eating after only a couple of bites. As the meal was ending, a gust of wind arose, tossing their napkins in the air.

"Let's go inside," he said, rising. "The weather's beginning to turn." Once in, Reid asked the waiter to bring them some iced tea. After they'd been served, Reid motioned for him to leave them alone.

"You're probably wondering what this is all about," he said taking a chair opposite Maddy, "so let me explain. Remember our last attempt at conducting an interview and the aide who rushed in telling me I had a call?"

Maddy nodded.

"It was the police. It was about Ray Trask, my chief engineer. He'd been missing for almost two weeks. He hadn't shown up at work and hadn't returned home. Obviously, everyone was frantic. Well, the morning of the call, the police found a car at the bottom of Riley Canyon, the same road you were on earlier today. It was Ray's car, completely destroyed and he was found dead behind the wheel. According to the police, he'd probably fallen asleep and driven over a cliff, possibly while on his way to see me."

"How awful. Were you close?"

"We'd been together for years." Reid replied. "He was one of my dearest friends."

"How critical was he to the Metrius project?"

"Invaluable."

"What a horrible accident."

Reid flashed a sardonic smile.

Noting his reaction, Maddy leaned forward with her elbows on her knees. "It *was* an accident, wasn't it?"

"I have my doubts."

Rising, Reid joined her on the couch. "Maddy, this is why I've asked you here today. I'm convinced that Ray was murdered."

Maddy stared back at Reid. "Murdered?" she exclaimed. "Are you sure?"

"Sure enough," he said. "But I can't prove it. Which is where you come in. I need you and your investigative resources to help me. The cops won't listen and I can't do it alone." Reid sighed. "I know I'm asking a lot, but if you promise to help me, I'll do something for you in return."

"Such as?"

"How do rights to the Metrius story sound? Not just the surface stuff, but the inside story of the deployments, from planning to execution, with access to all the principals."

"Exclusive rights?" Maddy asked.

"Yes."

Maddy eased back in her seat, unsure of how to respond. She was being offered an exclusive to the biggest news story of the decade. But covering it, at least according to Ed Snider, might cost her her job.

Sensing her unease, Reid asked her what was wrong.

Maddy explained her predicament. That Ed Snider threatened to fire her if she did anything other than sit at her anchor desk. Then with her mind on the importance of the story, she laughed ruefully. "Well, there are other jobs," she said. "This is too big for me to pass up. But before we go further, tell me something. The last time we spoke, you assured me that everything was going smoothly with the Metrius project. But today, I heard a news report that deployment has been pushed back a month."

Temple nodded slowly. "That's true."

"Why?"

"It was done at my request."

"Is this related to Ray Trask's death?"

"No," he replied, his eyes shifting away from Maddy's. "It's just routine testing issues," he muttered. "Nothing serious."

Watching his reaction, Maddy felt sure he was hiding something. She decided to switch tactics. "Why are you so sure Trask's death was murder and not simply an accident?"

"Before I answer, I need your guarantee that anything we discuss from this point on regarding Trask's death is strictly off-the-record. I do not want to turn on the news and hear you talking about it. Do I have your word?"

"And when my investigation is over, I'll get the Metrius story as an exclusive?"

Reid nodded.

"Okay," Maddy said, "it's off the record. So back to my question. Why do you doubt the police report?"

"In the weeks leading up to his death," Reid replied, "Ray was troubled by something. When I pressed him for details, he was deliberately vague, as if he didn't want to bother me with it. Around the same time, I saw something odd. I was leaving the office when I saw a car follow him from the company parking lot. It was car that I'd seen somewhere before, but didn't belong to any of the employees. When I later mentioned it to Trask, he nodded. He'd seen the car too and was convinced he was being tailed."

"Did he do anything about it?"

"He told me that he'd pulled over on a couple of occasions, trying to confront the person, but each time, the car passed without incident. Then, just when he felt he was imagining it all, the car would re-appear. Sometimes parked outside his house at odd hours, at others, suddenly popping up in traffic."

"Did he contact the police?"

"He told me he had, but when I spoke to them, they had no record of it."

Maddy shook her head. "Why would anyone follow Trask?" Then a thought jumped into her head. "Could this be related to Metrius? Perhaps someone trying to stop--"

"This has nothing to do with Metrius," Reid said sharply, cutting her off. "I'm just trying to get to the bottom of Ray's death." He looked at Maddy with a pleading in his eyes. "You've got the resources to look into this. I don't. Will you help?"

"I don't know," Maddy replied. "You've haven't given me much to go on. A car at the bottom of a canyon and someone possibly tailing Trask."

"I have nowhere else to turn."

Maddy sat for a moment. Though still convinced that Reid was hiding something, she nodded. "Okay, I'll give it a shot. The first step would be to scour his car for clues. I can set that up. Of course, I'll need to contact his wife and family and co-workers to see if they know anything."

Reid nodded. "I can arrange that."

From there, the conversation tailed off and the two sat quietly until Maddy's eyes fell upon the array of artifacts decorating the room, She asked where they were from.

South America Reid said. Had she'd ever visited Peru? Maddy shook her head.

"It's a fascinating place," he said, growing boyish and animated. For the next few minutes he regaled Maddy with stories of his trips, encounters with people of other cultures and his devotion to the environment. Impressed by his enthusiasm and his sincerity, Maddy, almost imperceptibly, felt herself softening toward him.

Then looking up, Maddy saw that the sky was darkening outside. She had to go. Before she did, she promised to keep him updated on her investigation into Trask's death.

Reid mentioned he was leaving for England the next day. Could he see her upon his return? To Maddy, it seemed like a silly question. She would see him when her investigation into Trask's death was completed. Or did he have something else in mind? Unsure of how to respond, Maddy smiled and said goodbye.

Chapter 12

A week following her meeting with Reid at the beach house, Maddy rang him at his office. She'd completed her investigation into Trask's death and was ready to share what she'd found. He was working long days he told Maddy and wouldn't be free until after hours. Could they meet over dinner, instead of at his office? When Maddy agreed, he suggested Antonio's, a favorite of his in Beverly Hills, the following evening at 7.

It was a warm spring evening when Maddy walked into Antonio's the next day. The restaurant, a popular eatery known for its pasta, was a darkened aisle of a place with a mirrored wall that strained to imbue the room with a feeling of space. Because she was a few minutes early, Maddy was surprised to find Reid Temple already seated at a table in a far corner of the room. As she approached, he rose and bade her good evening.

A moment later, a waiter approached. After perusing the menu, they ordered. Reid then asked about Maddy's investigation.

"Interviews with his family raised a lot of questions," Maddy said. "Apparently during the last four months of his life he spent virtually minute at work. Not just days, but sometimes all night too."

"He worked hard," Reid replied. "We all do."

Yes, Maddy said, but according to his family, this was different. He'd always worked diligently, but never around the clock. At first, his wife, thinking he was fooling around, accused him of having an affair, He convinced her that wasn't the case, but wouldn't say more. She also said that his personality had changed, from very upbeat to sullen and uncommunicative. Maddy, closely observing Reid's reaction, asked him what could account for such a change.

"I can't be sure," he replied in a small voice. "I can only assume he was feeling pressured to complete work on Metrius." Reid cleared his throat. "Did his wife know he was being followed?"

"No."

Reid asked about his car. Could anything be learned from that? Not really, Maddy replied. A forensic accident investigator that partnered with GBS news picked over the car from bumper to bumper, looking for evidence of the involvement of another person or vehicle. His conclusion? The car was so badly damaged from the steep fall into the canyon, it was impossible to tell if another vehicle might be involved.

"In short," Maddy said, "I could find no evidence of foul play."

Hearing her words, a faint expression of relief appeared on Reid's his face. "So that's it?" he asked.

"Not exactly," Maddy replied. "We did find something."

Reid stiffened. What was it?

"Something puzzled me about the crash," Maddy replied. "Trask's cell phone was not found in the car, which seemed strange. His wife assured me it was always with him. So where was it?"

"The police said the same thing," Reid said. "They assured me they'd looked high and low to find it."

"Well," Maddy said, "they didn't look hard enough. Because, after a few hours of scrounging around the crash site, we located it. Apparently it was thrown clear when the car tumbled down the grade. We found it about halfway down, wedged in a tree branch. And though the battery was low, it was still alive."

"Is this significant?"

"You bet. Because in the moments before he died, Trask was trying to text you."

"Me?"

"Yes. His partially completed message was still on his phone."

Reid stared back at Maddy with a stunned expression. "What did it say?"

Reaching in her purse, Maddy pushed a piece of paper across the table. When Reid picked it up, this is what he saw:

Ends just means tri ci

Reid eyed the note deeply for a long, silent minute.

"What did he mean, 'the ends just means'?" Maddy asked. "Does that refer to 'the ends justify the means'?"

"I assume so," Reid replied, "but I have no idea what the significance of that is." He shook his head. "I'm guessing he died before he could complete the text message."

As they puzzled over the strange message, the waiter arrived with simmering platters of ravioli in each hand. Reid, still gazing deeply at Maddy's note, appeared not to notice. Watching him, Maddy began weighing her feelings of guilt. Reid had promised her exclusive rights to the Metrius story -- access that other reporters would clamor for -- and all she had to offer in return was a cell phone with a few meaningless letters on it. Would he be angry?

"I won't hold you to our bargain," she said softly.

Reid, his concentration broken, glanced up. "Our bargain?" he asked.

"The Metrius exclusive," Maddy replied.

Reid waved a hand dismissively. "Don't be silly," he replied. "A bargain's a bargain."

Maddy, her mind on Ed Snider and his threat to fire her if she pursued stories on her own, shook her head. "It doesn't make any difference, anyway," she said.

"What do you mean?"

"Well, my boss threatened to fire me if I chased my own stories."

Reid smiled. "Oh that," he said casually. "It's taken care of."

Maddy asked what he meant.

"After our meeting a week ago, I rang him up."

"Who?"

"Ed Snider." Reid grinned. "It's funny, you said how difficult he was, but when he heard it was me on the phone, he was an absolute pussycat. Anyway, I told him that the real story of Metrius had yet to be told and you were the one to tell it." Reid smiled again. "For some reason, he couldn't agree more."

Maddy couldn't believe what she was hearing.

"So that's it," Reid said. "You have exclusive access to the Metrius story, from start to finish."

"But it's not fair," Maddy sputtered, "why should you—"

"Well, for one, I stood you up, what two times?"

"Three."

"Okay, three times. Second, with you handling the exclusive, I'm confident the story of Metrius will be told correctly." He reached for his fork and dug into his ravioli. "And third, well, I guess I like you." After flashing a boyish grin that erased the worry lines in his face, Reid signaled for the waiter and ordered a bottle of wine.

"So, I'll tell you what," he said, continuing. "Why don't you plan on coming to my place for dinner next week? Littleton will be there and you can get acquainted. After all, you'll need his cooperation. What do you say?"

Maddy smiled deeply, "Of course I'll be there," she said, then reached for the paper containing Trask's aborted text message to put it into her purse. Reid waved her off.

"You never know," he said tucking the note into his shirt pocket, "this might come in handy,"

At work the next day, Maddy felt at odds with herself. It seemed clear that Reid was interested. Not just in Metrius and how it would be reported in the press, but *in her*. From the beginning, their path had strewn with obstacles. She thought of how far things had come since then. From a series of misunderstandings and aborted interviews to a career-making assignment any news hound would covet. Maybe they'd been brought together for a reason, she mused to herself. Maybe, just maybe, she was falling for him. Then as quickly as the thought entered her head, she swatted it away. *Hadn't she learned that lesson?*

It wasn't just her doubts about men. There were other considerations. She knew that dating a source could jeopardize the thing she most valued: her career. Reid may have opened up to her regarding the death of his partner, but it was also clear that he was hiding something. Until she knew what it was, she was determined to keep her guard up. And of course, she couldn't disregard her past history. The fact was, she didn't fully trust any man and that included Reid Temple.

When she arrived at Reid's beach house on Saturday, she was amazed to see the elaborate preparations he'd made for the gathering. The house was laden with fresh flowers, while a chef and full staff readied food and drinks in preparation for the guests. Maddy, who viewed Reid as imperturbable, watched with amazement as he scurried from one room of the house to another, straightening and organizing. At eight o'clock, Littleton Barry, dapper and elegant, arrived in a chauffeured limousine with a dazzling twenty-ish brunette clinging to his arm. Trailing closely behind was Jason DeMir clutching a bottle of Dom Perignon, a laptop and a briefcase bulging with paper.

Once inside, Reid introduced Maddy to Barry. "Littleton," he said, "this is the woman I've been telling you about. The person who will share the full story of Metrius with the world."

"Pleased to meet you Mr. Barry."

"It's Littleton," he said softly tapping the tip of her nose with an index finger. After telling her he never missed her newscast, he congratulated her on becoming part of the team.

Barry turned to Reid with an expression of delight. "Can you believe it? In just three months we'll be on-line in the United States, France and the United Kingdom!"

Maddy watched curiously as Reid smiled weakly and said nothing.

"I've brought Jason along," Barry said, apparently taking no notice of Reid's subdued reaction. "I thought we could go over some details after dinner."

Dinner was served at eight and Maddy, who Reid had made sure would be seated next to Barry, immediately began to pepper him with questions regarding Metrius. When the queries grew intense, he laughed. "I hadn't expected a grilling over dinner," he said. "Why don't you contact my office next week and I'll tell you everything you want to know."

Following dinner, the group gathered outside on the deck for aperitifs. Above, the moon, framed by a luminous string of cumulus clouds, threw its light on the sea, while smoke curled from a brick chimney, sweetening the salt air with the scent of burning cedar. Maddy glanced over at Reid, who enthusiastically was regaling Littleton and his date with stories of adventures and misadventures south of the border. From the minute she'd arrived, he'd been attentive and charming, seeing to her every need and putting her at ease. The thought that she'd tried so hard to banish –that maybe they'd been brought together for a reason –again arose in her head.

Then, just minutes later, something happened to chase any such thoughts away. Reid, excusing himself to check on something, entered the house. Maddy deciding she needed to wash up, passed the study on her way toward the bathroom. Hearing a commotion coming from the room, Maddy looked in and saw that Reid, with teeth clenched and a fiery look in his eyes, had one of the waiters pinned against a wall. Maddy watched as Reid spat words at the frightened man, who was struggling to break free. After a minute had passed, Reid, still unaware of Maddy's presence, released him and the waiter bolted out the front door. A minute later, the squeal of tires could be heard as he raced from the house.

Startled by the confrontation, Maddy forgot all about her trip to the bathroom and entered the study, where she found Reid breathing heavily.

"What was that all about?"

Startled at seeing her, Reid shook his head. "Just a disagreement," he said, smoothing the front of his shirt. "Nothing serious."

"It sure looked serious."

"No," he said, an edge creeping into his voice. "Don't worry."

When the party finally broke up at midnight, Reid stood at the door and said goodbye to his guests. Maddy, who had just retrieved her coat from the bedroom was just about to exit when Reid placed his arm softly on her shoulder. "Won't you stay a little longer?" he asked.

Shaking her head, Maddy said goodbye. As she drove home, questions filled her head. What was the clash with the waiter about? What was Ray Trask trying to tell Reid in the moments before he died? Why did he react so strangely when Littleton Barry boasted about the upcoming Metrius deployments? And most importantly, what was he hiding?

Chapter 13

In the days following the dinner party, Maddy spent an increasing amount of time with Littleton Barry, unveiling her plan for a one-hour prime-time news special to air just prior to the Metrius deployments. To Maddy's surprise, it was an idea that Ed Snider willingly, if not enthusiastically, green-lighted. During Littleton's frequent trips out of town, Jason DeMir, as his lieutenant, acted as the liaison between Maddy and the Metrius development team, arranging interviews with key members to share their stories with her. The one exception was Reid Temple. Maddy knew his participation would be critical to the program, but the ugly scene with the waiter days earlier had lingered in her mind and she was in no hurry to renew contact. But finally the day came when in need of information that only Reid could provide, she called. He sounded delighted to hear from her. Maddy asked if they could meet to discuss issues related to Metrius. Sure, he replied, but it would have to take place at the beach house. Something about construction work at the office. Would Saturday be okay? After hesitating for a moment, Maddy agreed.

When she arrived late Saturday morning, work began in earnest, with discussions centering on how best to cover technical issues critical to the Metrius in a way that wouldn't cause viewers eyes to glaze over. To Maddy's surprise, Reid proved adept at distilling complex topics into simplified, yet informational nuggets that wouldn't short-change the technical side, yet be interesting enough to hold their audience's attention. They worked intensely for six hours, until Reid, feeling restless and in need of a break, suggested they take a walk on the beach. When Maddy agreed, Reid ducked down the hallway and returned with a battered backpack.

"What's that?" Maddy asked, her eyes on the worn and tattered bag in his hand.

"It's something I always take when I walk," he replied. "You never know when you might need it."

Suggesting that they walk in a southerly direction toward some tide-pools, they set off at a moderate pace. They'd walked a little more than a half-mile when Maddy spotted something unusual. It was an injured cormorant huddled against some large rocks lining the coastline. She motioned to Reid. "Did you see that? We walked to within a couple of feet of that bird and he never moved."

Turning Reid nodded. "Let's have a look."

Edging nearer, they saw that the bird was listless and sick. He had a fishhook embedded in the corner of his bill.

Maddy turned toward Reid. "He's really in trouble. Can we help him?"

"I don't know," he replied. "He's sick, but he's still got that sharp bill to rely on if he thinks we're getting too near. Tell you what. You try to distract him and I'll sneak up behind him. If you can hold his attention, maybe I can grab him and work the hook free."

Adopting a casual stride, Reid moved past the bird, then turned and tip-toed up behind him. All the while, Maddy spoke in low, soothing tones to the sick animal. Then in a flash, Reid lunged for the animal's neck, grabbing him squarely, then reached around with his left hand to seize the shocked bird's long beak. The startled animal fought frantically, but his weakened state prevented him from struggling free.

"God, look at the lice!"

Maddy pointed at a swarm of insects that had jumped from the bird's body and raced up Reid's arm the second that he made contact with the injured animal.

"Rats leaving a sinking ship," he muttered through locked teeth.

"I'm going to try and remove the hook. There's some peroxide in the backpack. Get it out, will you? And hurry, I can feel those damn lice working their way up my body."

Using a gentle back and forth motion, Reid managed to work the hook loose from the bird's bill. Then after dousing the injury with disinfectant, he eased the sick bird back to the sand. The stunned animal stumbled for a moment, then regained his balance and after emitting a shrill squawk at his rescuers, skittered away.

"You think he'll be ok?" Maddy asked.

"Hard to tell. Depends on how long that thing was in his mouth. It's been awhile since he's been able to eat. But at least he's got a fighting chance now."

Maddy, noticing deep scratches on Reid's arms, reacted with alarm. "Reid, you're bleeding."

Reid nodded. "Yeah, he cut me up good, didn't he?"

"They're pretty deep. You'll probably have scars," Maddy said.

"I've had worse….." Suddenly, he began to squirm. "Jeez!"

"The lice!" Maddy exclaimed. "Quick, give me your clothes, and then go jump in the water and see if you can't get those disgusting things off you."

Stripping off his shirt and shorts, Reid dashed madly for the shoreline clad only in his briefs. He hit the ocean at a horizontal angle, then surfaced and began to scrub himself frantically. After a minute or two, he emerged from the water and made his way over to where Maddy was waiting for him. As he approached, she burst out laughing.

"What's so funny?" Reid asked, annoyance in his voice.

"You should've seen yourself. The great Reid Temple, down to his skivvies, running like a wildman for the water. I'm sorry, but it's about the funniest thing I've ever seen." She burst out laughing again.

Noting his look of disapproval, she tried to stifle her laughter, but when she saw that his boxer shorts, weighed down with water and sand, were hanging at half-mast, her resolve broke and she fell to her knees laughing even harder.

Feeling ridiculed, Reid began to lecture her in a stern voice.

"Young lady, this is no laughing...." Then, realizing just how ridiculous he must look, his composure broke and he fell to the ground where he seized Maddy with a playful grab, their bodies a whirl of arms and legs and flying sand.

After catching her breath, Maddy asked Reid if he'd managed to get the lice off of him. "I don't know," he said. "Here, shake my hand and let's find out." Recoiling in mock horror, Maddy fell back to the sand laughing, where she remained for a minute, watching him as he dressed, a growing warmth reflected in her eyes. His attempts at saving the injured bird had impressed her, rekindling the affection she felt for Reid prior to the scene with the waiter. Her wall of resistance, which she'd erected brick-by-brick over the past weeks, was starting to crumble. Reid, who was shaking his shorts in an attempt to clear the sand said "I think I've figured out why they use beach sand to make sandpaper. Man, am I getting raw!"

Once back home, Reid quickly showered and they resumed work. So engrossed were they, that Maddy, upon looking up sometime later, saw that the sun had set. Getting to her feet and gathering up her notes, she told Reid she had to go.

Standing, Reid took her by the hand. "I can think of two reasons why you shouldn't," he said.

Maddy smiled. "Ok," she said, "let's hear them."

"Reason number one is Riley Canyon. Too dangerous to drive after dark."

"I'll concede that point," Maddy said. "What's number two?"

With a softness showing in his eyes, Reid smiled sheepishly. "The most important one of all. I want you to stay."

All the questions that Maddy usually asked herself at times like this --Is this right? Should I do this? What does it mean? -- were suddenly far away. "Well," she said, "maybe for a few minutes."

Flashing a smile, Reid made his way to a cabinet where he started some music. Soon, the midnight blue tones of Miles Davis filled the room. A moment later, he pulled a bottle from a wine rack, opened it and filled two glasses, handing one to Maddy.

After sipping from his glass, Reid leaned closer and traced his hand over Maddy's forehead and down the curve of her face. A moment later, Maddy felt his hand on her neck as he gently eased her hair back and placed his lips on the curve of her throat. As he did, Maddy felt a surge of warmth sweep up from below her navel flooding the rest of her body, With her resistance melting, Maddy went limp against him. With energy from her body now pouring into his, Reid placed his hands on her shoulders and with a gentle nudge, eased her back onto the cushion. Then lowering himself to the floor, he pressed the length of himself against her. As his lips met hers, Maddy reached out and began undoing the buttons of his shirt. When the garment finally yielded, the sculpted muscles of his chest were exposed to her exploring hands.

For the next hour, Reid loved Maddy intensely and unselfishly. Caressing her body as if it were his to possess, he stoked her desire, bringing her to the edge of release time and again before easing her back down again. When Maddy could finally stand no more, she seized a handful of Reid's hair and arched herself toward him. A moment later, she circled the small of his back with both hands and pulled him toward her with a forceful motion, desperate to get the full length of him inside her. As he did, Reid fixed her gaze upon her, and then, with his dark eyes flashing, he maneuvered his muscular hips expertly and brought each of them to a thunderous, powerful climax.

When it was over, Maddy propped an arm beneath her head and turned to face him.

"That was wonderful."

"Yeah, I'm a tiger." Reid studied Maddy's face for a moment through unsmiling eyes, then burst into a hail of self-deprecating laughter. As he gazed into the fire, Maddy studied him intently through narrowed eyes. The photos of him in magazines and newspapers hardly did the man justice, she thought. His profile, bathed in the orange-yellow glow of ebbing firelight, was almost sculptor perfect. Atop his head was a luxurious swatch of blue-black hair with a untamed forelock that insistently fell over his high forehead. His patrician nose and thin lips could make him appear stern, but years of joy were etched into the deep lines that framed his eyes when he laughed. His laugh was extraordinary; full, vociferous and robust, betraying not a trace of self-consciousness.

Suddenly, Maddy found herself thinking about the other women in his life; wondering just how many others had gazed upon that beautiful profile and looked at him just as she was looking at him now. At that moment, with the crackling fire and the smooth tones of Miles Davis as the only sounds in the room, her eyes fell upon a bookcase at the far side of the room. There in a silver frame, was a picture of Reid with another woman. In a flash, she bolted upright. Had she been a fool? Was another man about to disappoint her?

Watching her reaction, Reid smiled. "It's my wife. She died two years ago."

Chagrined, Maddy eased back to the floor. "I'm sorry. Do you want to talk about it?"

"There's not much to say. It was asthma."

"Are you ok?"

"Now? Yeah. But the first year? Not so hot."

Just before they retired for the evening, Maddy, unable to quell her journalist tendencies, raised the issue of the waiter and the troubling scene in the study. Like the cut of a scythe, Reid's happy mood evaporated and a black silence pierced the room. It was a long minute before he spoke.

"He wasn't a real waiter. He was here for something else."

Maddy was confused. "Here for what?"

For what seemed like minutes, Reid sat mute, obviously not wanting to say more. Maddy, feeling guilty for ending their day on such a sour note, quickly apologized.

Then, as if by magic, the dark spell was broken. With his mouth suddenly wearing a broad smile that left his eyes untouched, Reid sprang to his feet with catlike ease and extended a hand to Maddy. "Listen," he said, "everything's fine. There's nothing to worry about." He glanced at the clock over the fireplace. "Did you realize it's 1 o'clock?" We'd better hit the hay. Ready?"

Stunned by this latest shift in Reid's mood, Maddy said nothing. She grasped his hand, and he lifted her from the floor to his side, then hand-in-hand, the two of them made their way down the hall into the bedroom. She was troubled by Reid's strange behavior, but also was feeling the effects of the long day on her tired body and mind. Once she was in bed, it took just seconds for a deep and peaceful slumber to envelop her.

Sometime around 3 a.m., the cry of a gull outside the window jolted Maddy awake. After recognizing the source of the disturbance, she fluffed her pillow, then turned over and prepared to fall back asleep. Just before she did, she obeyed an impulse and glanced over at Reid.

What she saw stunned her. Instead of being asleep, he was fully awake and lying on his back, his eyes wide and fixed on the ceiling, the features of his handsome face twisted into a mask of anguish and despair that she sent an icy chill flashing down her spine.

Chapter 14

Over the next two weeks, Maddy, though still harboring a lingering distrust for men, saw more of Reid. As days passed, her resistance began to melt and her time at the beach house increased exponentially. By late spring, she began to eagerly anticipate their weekends together, which officially commenced when she arrived Friday night and usually didn't end until she departed for work late Monday morning. Daytimes usually meant a late breakfast, then a walk; sometimes to the north past the smattering of beach homes that dotted the sand or, most preferable, to the south where they encountered open beach, coves and natural rock formations. It had almost become a ritual; once breakfast was over and the dishes were done, Reid would turn to Maddy and ask "How about a walk?" Then just before heading out the door, he would bolt down the hallway for the battered backpack that acted as equal parts storage space, refreshment center and first aid kit. Maddy, amazed at the variety and utility of items that Reid pulled from the pack, had taken to calling it the "magic bag." One day in early June when Reid was feeling especially frisky and pulled Maddy down behind a sand dune to make love, he even managed to produce an old blanket for them to lie on. Afterward, when they were both exhausted, Maddy could only shake her head in amazement as Reid triumphantly pulled a pair of cold beers from the bag to toast the moment.

As time passed and her resistance to him faded, she lost count of the qualities in him that pleased her. Her initial attraction had been his looks and his intelligence. Later she discovered his sense of humor; time and again he'd reduce her to hysterics with biting and sardonic observations of everyday events that he piled one on top of another until her ribs ached and she was left gasping for air. As more time passed, she came to treasure his small eccentricities. She adored the childlike way he'd stop to tuck a fresh handkerchief into the rear pocket of his pants before ever leaving the house, how he couldn't pass a dog without stopping to make friends and his excitement at sharing a favorite old movie with her.

It was only as the deployment date for the Metrius plants approached that the closeness between them was shattered. Increasingly, he'd toil silently and to Maddy's mind, secretively behind the door of his study for hours. Sometimes the phone would ring, and Maddy would hear his muted voice filtering through the shuttered door. At other times, the room would fall silent for long periods. What most disturbed her was the odd behavior he exhibited when he emerged from his office in late afternoon. She first noticed it in mid-June when she was in the kitchen putting away groceries.

"Hi," she said to Reid as he entered the room. " I just got back from the store. Are you done for the day? If so, maybe we can...."

Ignoring her, Reid made his way to the refrigerator, then, after withdrawing a beer, he turned on his heel and wordlessly left the kitchen. Startled by his behavior, Maddy dumped her canned goods to the kitchen counter and charged after him. By the time she reached the living room, Reid had already exited the house and was making his way across the sand toward the shoreline. For the next sixty minutes, Maddy stood at the window and watched as Reid paced the sand, looking for all the world like he was trying to divine the solution to an insoluble riddle. Finally, after an hour of the anguished to and fro, he returned to the house.

"Hi," he said bursting through the front door with a wide grin. "How about a walk?"

"First things first," Maddy replied evenly. "What's going on?"

"Nothing. Why?"

"Oh, I dunno," Maddy replied. "An hour ago you blew by me in the kitchen like I wasn't there. Since then, I've watched you wear down the sand in front of the house. Why would I think anything was wrong?"

"Oh that," Reid replied with a wave of his hand. "It's nothing. Just work, that's all. You know, Metrius." Then with a softness showing in his face, he approached her. "Forgive me for ignoring you," he said planting a soft kiss on her forehead. "It wasn't intentional. I just have a lot going on right now." Then with a comic regality, he bowed deeply and gestured toward the beach. "Madam!" he exclaimed, his voice clipped and proper, "There's a great day going on out there and we're missing it. How about a walk?"

Unable to stop her face from breaking into a wide grin, Maddy nodded. In a flash, Reid dashed down the hallway to retrieve the magic bag, while Maddy, still puzzling over this latest mood shift, stared out the window. To her, Reid's actions were a discordant echo of his strange behavior she'd witnessed earlier. In many ways, Reid was transparent; he laughed when he felt happy, cried was he was sad, and through it all, seemed to be playing straight with her. That he was tormented by something was obvious. That he was unwilling to confide in her was equally apparent. Still, Maddy clung to his reassurances, and over the next few days nearly succeeded in convincing herself that everything was fine with the man she had come to admire. That is, until one day when a strange series of events revealed to her just how much was at stake.

It was a sun-washed day in the third week of June and weather reports spoke of an offshore flow. That usually signaled a warm, fog-free day and Maddy and Reid had planned to explore some tidepools a mile to the south. By the time they left the house, it was just 10:30, but already the temperature hovered near the ninety-degree mark. As they made their way across the sand, Maddy, her interest fired by the Metrius plants that were scheduled to go online in less than three weeks, prodded Reid for an update on how things were going. Reid, who was gazing out at the ocean, calmly began to inform Maddy of the latest on the deployments when suddenly his voice trailed off. Reacting to his silence, Maddy looked up and saw Reid, a startled expression on his face, staring intently at something just over her right shoulder.

Turning, Maddy spied a powerfully built man in wrap-around sunglasses standing atop a bluff overlooking the beach. He wore a loud yellow sport coat and burgundy doubleknit slacks, the kind that hadn't been in style for twenty years. He appeared to be staring directly at them.

Maddy turned toward Reid. "You know that guy?" Reid made no reply.

To Maddy, an eternity seemed to tick by before the mysterious man stepped back from the bluff then with a deliberate, taunting gait, made his way to an unusually painted tan and black car and drove away.

Reid, his voice suddenly cheerful, broke the silence. "Ok, let's go."

Maddy eyed him sternly. "How oblivious do you think I am?

He looked at her, a pained expression on his face. "Ok. Things are a little strange right now. But I don't want to talk--

"We will talk about it," Maddy replied, cutting him off. "And now."

Reid, his gaze fixed on the sand, remained silent.

Suddenly embarrassed at her willingness to believe in this man, Maddy pushed him away, turned on her heel and started for the beach house. A minute later, Reid caught up with her and pulled her into a lingering hug. "I need you to trust me," he said, a pleading in his eyes.

That night, they managed to hide the tension between them as they hosted Mako and a new boyfriend for a barbecue on the deck. The gathering didn't end until 1 am and Reid and Maddy slept until nearly nine the following morning. While Reid made the bed, Maddy went outside for the morning paper.

Stepping down from the porch, Maddy was enveloped in a heavy, dank fog that had swept in during the night. Cinching her robe tightly against her neck, she was seized by an eerie feeling that she was being watched. Attempting to shake off the uneasiness, she reached for the paper, then started back toward the house. As she did, a momentary shift in the fog made Maddy aware of something shimmering at the end of the driveway. She stopped and stared hard, but the wet gray shroud shifted again, obscuring her view. A moment later the fog yielded, affording Maddy a brief, but clear sightline to the area that bordered the road. Faintly visible through the shifting soup, she saw a uniquely colored sedan parked at the top of the driveway. And sitting behind the wheel was a bull-necked man in wrap-around sunglasses.

With her senses at full alert, Maddy ran to the house where she found Reid in the kitchen preparing coffee. After dropping the newspaper on the kitchen counter, she approached him. "Remember that car from yesterday? It's parked on the road. And that weird guy is behind the wheel. What the hell is going on?"

Reid stepped to the window. "Go ahead and have your breakfast," he said pulling the curtain aside and peering out the window. "I've got some things to do."

Reid walked quickly to his study. Maddy assumed he was calling the police, but a half hour passed and no one came to the door. When Maddy looked out the window a short time later, she saw that the strange car was gone. When she went to tell Reid, she found him in the hallway, yanking a suitcase from a closet that he promptly carried into the bedroom and dropped on the bed. Without uttering a word to Maddy, he criss-crossed the room, pulling shirts and pants from hangers, then one-by-one stuffing them in the bag. To Maddy, it was bad enough that they were being stalked by a strange man, but to have Reid stonewall her was inexcusable. Enough was enough. She wanted answers and she would have them. She charged into the bedroom and stood directly in front of Reid, who was shoving some socks into a corner of his suitcase.

"Look, we've got some weirdo camped out in our driveway, watching us like we're specimens in a jar or something. Enough intrigue. I want to know what the hell's going on."

Reid, who was struggling to zip the suitcase, smiled wanly. When the bag was finally secured, he reached for her hand and led her into the living room. After motioning her toward the couch, he sat down beside her.

"I've been contacted by someone I have to see."

"So pick up the phone."

"I can't."

"Are you saying our phone's been tapped?"

"I won't be gone long. With luck, I can clear this up in a day or two."

"Well that's clear as mud," she said, fixing him with an icy glare. "Reid, what are you keeping from me?"

"I'm being as honest as I can with you."

His response cut through her like a rock dropping through water. "That's bullshit," Maddy blurted, her anger flashing. For the next few moments, she scavenged for words she hoped might reach him. "Don't you get it?" she asked finally. "We're supposed to be a team-

--"

He covered Maddy's lips with his hand, silencing her protests. His eyes, always strong and unyielding were now soft. When he opened his mouth to speak, she was shocked at what she heard.

"Maddy, I love you."

Stunned, Maddy stared at him through widened eyes. A moment later, she started to speak. "Reid, I –" But then, with emotion swelling in her chest, her words were choked off.

"It's funny," Reid said, a faraway look now in his eyes. "I never expected to say those words to a woman ever again." He rose from the couch. "But I've got to leave. In the meantime, you'd better go home."

Maddy jumped to her feet. "Reid, please tell me what's going on!"

He pulled something from his shirt pocket and pressed it into Maddy's hand.

"What's this?" she asked staring at the gleaming object in her palm.

"It's a tribal good luck charm. It was given to me by a Quechua peasant on one of my treks to South America. It's hundreds of years old. It supposedly has mystical powers." He laughed a small laugh. "That probably sounds silly, but it's always carried it with me and it's brought me good luck. I want you to have it."

Maddy nodded, then after exhaling deeply, reached up to brush away the forelock that had tumbled over his forehead. He kissed her, then, cradling her face with his hands, smiled deeply at her. "I love you, always remember that. And I'll see you soon." He then reached for his suitcase and made his way toward the door. Then after stopping briefly in the hallway for a fresh handkerchief that he stuffed in his back pocket in that little boy way of his, he was gone.

Chapter 15

On the day following Reid's departure, Maddy did her best to stay busy. On Tuesday, she was in her office skimming through her email when something caught her eye. There it was again, the same message she'd been receiving for weeks:

"I have knowledge of an imminent terrorist plot against this country."

--Constant Viewer

Thinking that some people had too much time on their hands, Maddy deleted the strange message. A moment later, her cell rang. To her relief, it was Reid. He was in Northern California. Silicon Valley, he told her. He was meeting with someone tonight who could clear things up. He'd be home soon, probably in a day or two. Then he would explain everything. To Maddy, he sounded relieved, as if a dark burden had been expelled from his life. Just before he hung up, he promised to call the following day.

On Wednesday, a haze that was neither fog nor clouds clung to the sky, dampening Maddy's mood. The work day passed without word from Reid and when she tried his cell, she got no answer. That night the only person who called was Mako.

On Thursday morning, she was leaving a production meeting when she noticed Mako and a group of co-workers standing in a half circle staring wide-eyed at a bank of TV monitors.

"Maddy! Maddy!" Mako screamed upon seeing her. "Come here! Hurry!"

When she approached she saw the group was listening to a bulletin from the GBS headquarters in New York. As she drew near, she was stunned at what she heard.

"In a shocking development, Palo Alto police have named tech pioneer and author Reid Temple has their prime suspect in the case. The woman, who has not yet been identified pending notification of her relatives, was brutally beaten in her home sometime in the early hours of Wednesday morning. According to a manager in whose restaurant they were seen, Temple dined with the woman Tuesday evening and they left together at around midnight. Neighbors of the woman reported hearing a disturbance sometime after 1am and the sound of a woman's scream, but did not summon police. Temple, a co-developer of Metrius, the revolutionary nuclear energy source that is scheduled to be deployed in three countries in just weeks, could not be located by police and has apparently fled the city. Again, tech nova Reid Temple is being sought for questioning in the murder of a young woman in Northern California. We'll have more details later on this breaking story."

When the report ended, Maddy, with Mako by her side, made their way toward Maddy's office. As they passed, Ashley Stevens muttered to a co-worker "Should be fun listening to her newscast tonight."

Entering Maddy's office, Mako closed the door and faced her friend. "Maddy," she said, "have you heard from Reid?"

Maddy, zombie staring at the carpet, said nothing.

"Maddy?"

"Sorry," Maddy said raising her eyes, "what did you say?"

"Have you heard from Reid?"

"No. It's been two days since he left for Silicon Valley. I tried to reach him all day yesterday and last night and I kept getting his voice mail. I've pleaded with him to call me, but….."

"The whole thing's insane," Mako said. "Reid beating a woman to death? Absurd, completely absurd."

Maddy nodded. "Or course it is. But why haven't I been able to reach him?"

"What's he doing in Silicon Valley?"

"He wouldn't say. He just left suddenly on Sunday, didn't tell me where he was headed. When I spoke to him on Monday, he told me he was in Palo Alto, thought it would take a day or two to clear up some issues and he'd be home."

"Do you know the woman he was with?" Mako asked, treading lightly.

"No," Maddy said reaching for her cell and punching in Reid's number. A moment later she flung the phone to her desk. "No answer. Nothing." A long silent moment passed with Maddy lost in thought. Then she spoke. "Will you run down to the beach house with me? I may not find anything to explain what's going on, but it's worth a try. What do you say?"

At that moment, a production aide burst into the office informing Maddy that the police were in the lobby waiting to speak with her.

After brushing back a wisp of hair that'd fallen in her face, Maddy nodded, then told Mako they'd leave as soon as she was done speaking with them.

For the ensuing few minutes, the police peppered Maddy with questions. Why was Reid in Silicon Valley? Did she know who he was meeting with? After answering 'no,' the police sergeant delivered the kicker. "We know you've been meeting with Temple regularly. Why?"

"Who told you that?" Maddy asked, her eyes narrowing.

"That doesn't matter," the sergeant replied. "I want to know why you've been seeing Temple."

"To prepare a news special on the Metrius nuclear deployments," Maddy replied icily.

"We'll need your notes."

"Why?"

"This is a murder investigation. We're pursuing every lead."

"Sorry. They're protected. A little matter concerning the First Amendment."

"A court order might change your mind."

Maddy shook her head defiantly. "It won't."

"Then maybe some jail time will," the sergeant replied. "You'll be hearing from us." Then motioning to his partner, the two left. Ten minutes later, she and Mako departed for the beach house.

The weather was clear and bright when they left, but as the coastline drew near, blue skies gave way to low clouds. By the time they exited the freeway and entered Riley Canyon, a cold, clammy fog was shrouding the entire coastline.

As they approached the beach house, they saw that a teeming

crowd of reporters was gathered outside, held back by a cordon of police. After identifying themselves to an officer at the front door, Maddy expected to be granted access, but the cop shook his head. No one gets in, he said. Calmly, Maddy insisted on speaking with the officer in charge. When he approached, Maddy explained who they were. "Doesn't matter," he said. "Temple's a murder suspect. No one gets in until our investigation is done."

Peering over his shoulder into the living area of the house, Maddy was stunned by what she saw. The house had been completely ransacked, with books and papers ripped from shelves and dumped in a pile in the middle of the floor. Even the couch had been upended, four legs jutting upward like stunted spokes.

"Does investigating a murder case," Maddy said, "give you the right to turn the place upside down?"

The officer shook his head. "That's the way we found it. When we arrived, the front door was wide open and the place had been completely worked over."

The house had been burglarized? Maddy couldn't believe it. Stepping down from porch, she dashed to the side of the house and peered in the window to Reid's study. From where she stood, she saw that every piece of furniture had been pushed over; books were torn from their shelves and every file cabinet drawer in the room had been yanked free and their contents strewn about the room. Returning to the front door, Maddy asked once again to be admitted. Absolutely not, came the response. A moment later, when the cop guarding the door was distracted, Maddy ducked in and pulled

Reid's backpack from the hall closet.

"This was no ordinary burglary," Maddy said, as she and Mako made their way back to their car.

"What do you mean?"

"Think about it," Maddy said. "What kind of burglar rifles through file cabinets?"

"Hey, that's right," Mako exclaimed, a look of wonder in her eyes. "I wonder if he found what he was looking for."

It was then that Mako noticed that Maddy was clutching something in her hand.

"What's that?" she asked as she revved the car's engine.

"It's Reid's backpack. I snatched it when the cops weren't looking. It's silly I guess. But he was so attached to it, I thought I'd bring it with me."

"What's that thing sticking out of the side?"

Flipping the bag around, Maddy spied a slip of paper protruding from one of its folds. Yanking the paper free, Maddy saw that it was in Reid's handwriting:

"RFHF. Get to RS before they do!"

Chapter 16

The lone figure hiked to the edge of the brush-lined trail, a wall of rock towering behind him. His path had taken him to the edge of a precipice and he peered out over the edge to the flat deck of the desert floor far below. From where he stood he could see a string of palm groves - a strip of green that zig-zagged its way through the jagged landscape of Cahuilla Canyon and stretched on into the horizon. The sweat that cascaded from his neck had made his shirt stick to his back and after wiping his brow, he reached for his canteen. As he gulped the cool water, he glanced at the sun that burned overhead. It was hard to believe that it was only June. Going to be a brutal summer. After dousing himself with water, he hitched the canteen to his belt, then shot a glance over his shoulder. In the distance, he could just make out the faint outline of the trading post, where an hour earlier, he'd stopped for directions.

The woman behind the counter eyed him curiously. Cradle Rock? Was he sure he wanted to go there? It was a long way and the trail was rugged. Lonely too. Aside from the occasional rattlesnake, she said, you probably won't see a soul. Just too damn hot for most folks.

A thermostat bolted to an adobe wall outside said 108 degrees. Except for the wind in his ears, the only sound was the occasional cry of a red-tail hawk circling on a thermal just to the east. He glanced at his watch. The shopkeeper said it would take him just over an hour to get where he was going. He knew he must be getting close. Not only to Cradle Rock, but closer to solving the mystery that had consumed his life for the past six months.

The police were closing in on him, he knew that. He hadn't killed her, but in a way, maybe he had. If she wasn't seen with him in Palo Alto, she might still be alive. And he certainly wouldn't be here, hoping to solve a riddle that had darkened his life. Because however awful they may have been, the weeks of anguish he'd endured had finally produced a vital clue: he now understood what Trask was trying to tell him in the moments before he died.

He slung his canteen over his shoulder and resumed his journey. With his every footstep on the sun-baked trail, he thought of Maddy. Leaving without being able to tell her why tortured him. But it was for her own good. Her safety depended on her staying out of it. He also knew that she'd heard the news reports by now. Then, remembering what was at stake, he remonstrated himself.

Stay focused. Get this settled once and for all.

He'd be home in a couple of days and would fix everything. But for another brief moment, he allowed his mind to linger on the wonderful moment when they would be together again. Then suddenly, his thoughts were broken.

God, there it was. Just where she said it would be.

Maybe a half-mile away, partially obscured by a lush grove of date palms, he spotted it; a rectangular building sitting squat and low beneath the unforgiving desert sun. Surrounding it was a chain link fence topped with barbed wire and on the far side was a strip of two lane blacktop that wound its way from the facility to a hilly region of open desert far beyond. With cautious steps, he made his way to the very edge of the precipice, determined to get a good look at what those who were determined to destroy him had created.

In the grip of such concentration, it's not surprising that he didn't hear the crunching of gravel beneath the booted foot, didn't see the fatal shadow that darkened the boulder to his right. And didn't anticipate the dark figure that streaked toward him from behind, driving him toward the cliff edge and the vast distance below.

Chapter 17

Immediately after returning from the beach house, Maddy, desperate for anything that would solve the riddle of Reid's time in Palo Alto, contacted police asking for a copy of the police report. From the moment they'd met, Maddy had been conflicted over Reid Temple. Initial resentment over missed interviews had gradually given way to a growing respect as she witnessed first hand his devotion to Metrius and what it meant to the world. As more time passed, respect had morph'd into a powerful physical attraction, that despite her efforts, she couldn't quell. Through it all however, Maddy was unable to shake an undercurrent of suspicion. Reid's secrecy and moodiness had left her deeply troubled and the skirmish with the waiter continued to prey on her mind. Now with the death of the young woman in Palo Alto, a seed of uncertainty had been planted: Did she really know who Reid Temple was? Could it be possible that he'd actually killed that girl?

The arrival of the police report a few days later assuaged her doubts. According to the report, the dead woman was named Rita Sessions and she was a volunteer at something called the Relief From Hunger Foundation. Reading the words, Maddy's mind flashed back to the note she'd found in Reid's backpack.

RFHF. Get to RS before they do.

'RS' was obviously Rita Sessions! And RFHF referred to the Relief From Hunger Foundation! Reid, somehow having learned that Rita was in danger, had left for Silicon Valley in an attempt to prevent her from being harmed. It was now clear: Reid *couldn't have* killed that girl. In a flash, shame consumed Maddy. How could she for one moment thought he was capable of such a thing? Everything he was was on file somewhere in her mind: The brave visionary with dreams for a new world. The dedicated explorer, constantly in search of new horizon. The gentle man laboring to save an injured bird. The comical figure emerging from the surf with his underwear at half-mast. With a groan, her mind flashed back to the last time she saw him. When he spoke of his love for her, not as something that would be, but as something that *was*. Why had she been so cautious? She *did love* him, she knew that now. And she lived for the moment when she would see him again and finally be free to tell him exactly how she felt. In the meantime, she would work tirelessly – Ed Snider be damned - to clear his name.

For hours, Maddy remained at her desk, pouring over the police report for clues or inconsistencies. At 1 a.m, feeling exhausted and demoralized, she finally left her office and made her way to her car.

Arriving home, Maddy walked immediately to her telephone. Seeing that her message light was flashing, her hopes quickened, but fell when none of the messages turned out to be from Reid. Having not eaten since breakfast, she went to the kitchen, but quickly realized she had no appetite. Unsure of what to do with herself, she entered the den and stretched out on the couch. The room, which was positioned to absorb the late afternoon sun, was stiflingly hot despite the lateness of the hour. At a far corner, a dry wind swept in from an open window and blew the drapes against the wall with a rhythmic thwap, thwap, thwap. Emotionally and physically exhausted, it took only seconds for her to fall into a heavy slumber.

Sometime later, Maddy awoke with a start. Propping herself up on one elbow, she reached for the clock. 5 a.m. With a sigh, she fell back onto the couch, mulling whether to go into the bedroom and attempt to fall asleep again or stay where she was. Deciding that she'd slept enough and finally feeling hungry, she made her way through the pre-dawn darkness toward the kitchen.

The house was still and black, fueling the gnawing dread that always overcame Maddy just before sunrise. After retrieving a bagel and making herself a cup of instant coffee, she returned to the den and switched on the television to counter the foreboding silence of the house. As she absentmindedly stirred her coffee, she could hear the anchorwoman on CNN in the background, running down the latest headlines.

" *In Southern California, authorities have tentatively identified a body they found in the desert as tech giant Reid Temple. According to well-placed sources in the Palm Springs police department, Temple's death appears to be a suicide. Temple was being sought by police in the bludgeoning death of Rita Sessions, a charity worker in Palo Alto on Thursday. Again, the body of Reid Temple has been found in a remote corner of the Southern California desert, an apparent suicide. We'll have more details later on this breaking story."*

Maddy's body went limp as the room began to spin. She felt the coffee cup slip from her fingers, then heard it smash to the tile floor below. With light racing from her brain, she staggered crazily backwards, trying desperately to make it to the couch before she passed out.

For minutes, Maddy hung suspended between light and dark. Her eyes flickered and she slowly became aware that her cheek was pressed against something cool and hard. As light re-entered her brain, she realized that it was the tile floor of the den. Bracing her arms beneath her, she pushed herself to a sitting position, strands of hair cascading down her face. Her mouth was very dry and there was a painful spot on her the back of her head where she'd fallen. Unsure of how long she'd been out, she remained there waiting for her head to clear. Finally, head still spinning, she forced herself to her feet and with lurching steps, made her way to the bathroom.

Then the terrible news came flooding back. With a groan, she reached for the faucet and with her body slumped over the sink, splashed cold water into her face. Then with blood still throbbing in her temples, she made her way back to the den and reached for the remote. Skimming through the news channels, she heard something that made her stiffen. A reporter on a cable news stations was delivering a special report.

" Temple, one of the countries most successful entrepreneurs, has died in an apparent suicide. Police are theorizing that Temple, who was a fugitive sought by the police in the beating death of a young woman in Palo Alto, was found in a remote region of the Southern California desert after throwing himself from a cliff two hundred feet above the desert floor to his death."

In disbelief, Maddy screamed "No!" It didn't seem possible. To her, it was as if all rules governing reason and reality had somehow been suspended. In an act of denial, she skipped frantically from channel to channel, daring America's news sources to confirm Reid's death, then dying a little each time they did.

The phone rang, breaking her concentration. Glancing up, Maddy was stunned to see the sun was shining brightly outside. She picked up the phone and heard Mako's voice, distraught and anxious. "I just heard. Dear god!" After telling Maddy that she'd be over as soon as she could change her clothes, she hung up. Over the next hour, word of the terrible event spread and Maddy's phone began to ring incessantly. The most troubling was from Jason DeMir, whose tormented cries made it clear that he was devastated over the news.

Shortly after 8 am, Mako arrived. After a lingering embrace, the two women made their way into the kitchen where Maddy was about to brew some tea.

"God, how can this be?" Mako said. "It's just so horrible."

Maddy, who was struggling to remove a cellophane wrapper from a box of tea bags, looked up. "It's not true."

Mako flinched, her eyes narrowing to slits. "What do you mean? Are you saying that Reid is still alive?"

"No," Maddy replied, her attention still fixed on the tea box. "I mean about him committing…......Damn this thing!" Maddy, still unable to open the tea box, began jabbing a fingernail into the package.

"What do you mean?" Mako asked. "What's not true?"

"Well, if Reid's dead--" Suddenly Maddy spat out an expletive and with her frustration cresting, began slamming the tea carton against the counter. "Why the fuck can't I open this!"

Mako darted to her side, then after gently taking the box from her hands, eased an arm around Maddy's back. As she did, Maddy shoulders began to heave uncontrollably.

"Damn it! Just damn it!" Maddy shrieked, grief hanging from her like a weight. "Reid's dead! Can you believe that?" For the next few minutes, the two women remained linked, Maddy pouring out pain while Mako held her tightly. When she could cry no more, Mako lead her to the table and motioned for her to sit down.

After taking a minute to compose herself, Maddy leaned across the table toward Mako.

"Reid didn't kill that girl."

"Of course he didn't," Mako replied.

"And if he didn't kill her," Maddy said, beginning to trace little circles in her forehead with the fingers of her right hand, "then why would he kill himself? It makes no sense."

Mako stared at Maddy, her face tight. "What are you saying? That it was….."

"Right, murder."

"I guess that makes as much sense as anything that's happened the past few days. But what I don't understand, who'd want to kill Reid?

"Remember what happened at the beach house?"

"You mean the burglary?" Mako shot Maddy an uncomprehending look. "You're trying to say that whoever ransacked Reid's house also killed him?"

"I don't know. But there's been some strange things going on lately. I haven't told you everything because I didn't want you to worry."

"Like what?"

For the next thirty minutes, Maddy recounted the odd events of the past weeks. Of Trask's death, the disturbing figure on the cliff, of the car parked outside the beach house, and of course, of his sudden departure.

Maddy eyed her friend with a forlorn expression. "Mako, I let him down," she said, dabbing her eyes with a tissue. "Just before he left, he told me he loved me. And I just sat there, wanting to tell him the same thing, but for some reason I couldn't get the words out. What's wrong with me? How could I let him leave without telling him how I felt?"

Mako reached for her friend's hand.

"He knew how you felt. Please don't torture yourself."

As Maddy dabbed her eyes, Mako, her mind on what she'd just learned, leaned toward Maddy with lines on concern etched in her face. "Regarding all the strange things that happened before Reid left, why didn't you inform the police?"

"I did, most of it anyway," Maddy replied. "but they pooh-poohed it. They're convinced he was guilty. They think Reid was having some sort of affair with that woman that got out of hand."

"Are they investigating her background?"

"Yes and so am I. That'll take some time."

"I have a question," Mako said. "Do you think Reid was being completely honest with you over what was troubling him?

"No," Maddy replied. "But whatever it was, I'm convinced it was something to do with the project."

"Metrius?"

"Yes. But he was very tight-lipped over it all. No matter how much I dug, he told me nothing."

Mako then said she'd remembered something from the research Maddy was doing on Metrius. Wasn't someone from the University of Santa Cruz involved with the project? Maddy nodded.

"My dad teaches there," Mako said. "Maybe he can tell us who it was." Maddy, figuring it was long shot, nonetheless said ok.

With evening approaching and the house starting to close in on her, Mako suggested that they drive into Glendale for a light dinner. As they dined, Maddy suddenly shushed Mako.

"Listen. It's the TV. About Reid."

The women both turned to face a TV on in the bar where a news anchor was reading a statement from Littleton Barry. Everyone involved with Metrius was stunned over the loss of their friend and partner, he said. While they awaited further information regarding the matter, he wished to assure the world that the Metrius project, which promised to provide the planet with safe and unlimited nuclear energy, would continue without interruption, with the first plants scheduled to go on-line in just two weeks. That's something, Barry concluded, that Mr. Temple would have wanted.

Fighting tears, Maddy signaled to Mako that she wanted to leave. When they pulled up in front of Maddy's house, Mako angled herself to face her.

"Stay with me tonight," she said. "I've got a big empty bed with your name on it."

Maddy felt a sigh slip from her chest. "I'll be happier here, but I may call you later tonight. You know, just to talk."

After saying good night, Maddy made her way inside. With Mako gone and night falling, she became aware of how desolate the house felt. It was funny how much emptiness could be contained by four walls. Once inside, Maddy walked directly to the bedroom, convinced that sleep was the only way to shrink the thoughts that crowded her head. But once in bed, fearful thoughts descended and it wasn't until nearly daylight that a troubled sleep finally came to Maddy Daniel.

"Don't worry, I've got you."

Four days later, Jason DeMir, a protective arm wrapped tightly around her shoulders, guided Maddy toward the funeral home, where outside, a pack of reporters stirred excitedly. All efforts at keeping

Reid's services private had failed, and like jackals storming a fresh kill, the media had descended en mass on the mortuary, creating a chaotic scene. Immediately following the services, Jason and Maddy made their way back through the frenzied throng to Jason's car. An hour later, he dropped her off at Los Angeles International Airport where Maddy, after arranging an extended bereavement leave, hopped a flight home to spend time with her family. But instead of finding solace in Arizona, Maddy was stalked by howling, gnashing memories every day she was there.

On July 14th, Maddy, her fingers steepled into a pyramid of prayer, watched on TV as the first Metrius-enabled nuclear plant went on-line in the United States. Standing before the Poughkeepsie reactor at Indian Point, Littleton Barry addressed an enthusiastic crowd. "This is a great day, not just for the United States, but the world. For today, the future has arrived. For the first time in human history, Metrius will supply safe nuclear energy and a future free from the threat of global climate change." After acknowledging the dignitaries in attendance, Barry closed his remarks by saluting the efforts of his team and then uttered words that brought tears to Maddy's eyes. "Reid Temple was my friend and partner. Without his efforts, none of this would have been possible. While I await news that will completely clear him of complicity in recent unfortunate events, I want to world to know of his invaluable role in this great achievement. I am certain that he is with us in spirit today."

Following his remarks, Barry flipped a switch that took the nuclear power reactor at Poughkeepsie New York on-line. At the same moment, Sahn Rameer in London and President Guy Belcourt of France, surrounded by a large contingent of government officials and well-wishers, did the same. Metrius plants had now begun commercial operations in all three countries.

Minutes following the ceremony, a press release was issued from the energy departments of the United States, Great Britain and France. Energy was flowing smoothly from the Metrius plants to surrounding communities. In the words of Littleton Barry, a 'new epoch in human history' had begun.

Chapter 18

July 15th

After leaving Arizona, Maddy flew to Northern California on Saturday with the sole purpose of digging up as much information as she could on Rita Sessions. Her first stop was the neighborhood where she was killed. Knocking on doors and questioning neighbors revealed little. By all accounts, Rita was quiet and kept to herself. Her killing was a shock to everyone. Her next stop was the restaurant where Reid and Rita dined the evening she was killed. When she spoke to the waiter who served them that night, he said something that stunned her: There was a third person at the table with Reid and Rita that night!

"A third person?" Maddy replied, shocked. "Why hasn't anyone reported it?"

The police questioned his manager, the waiter said, but not him. As it turns out, the manager was in his office most of the night, and only came out once or twice. He'd probably seem Mr. Temple and Rita Sessions arrive together, the waiter said, but not a second man who showed up a few minutes later. And because the restaurant was otherwise empty, no one else had seen him either.

Could he describe the man?

Dark complexion, powerfully built, mid-40's, the waiter replied, with a bushy, grey-speckled beard. He stayed about thirty minutes, then left alone.

Was he able to overhear what they were talking about?

He shook his head. But it appeared to be a very serious conversation, he said. Lots of hushed voices and side-long glances.

After thanking him, Maddy weighed what she'd learned. Was the man at their table the person Reid referred to before he departed the beach house? Or was he talking about Rita Sessions? Maddy's thoughts then shifted to Rita and her role in the mystery.

Obeying an impulse, Maddy reached for her phone and dialed Palo Alto police. After identifying herself, she requested the phone number of Rita's immediate family. When she rang the number a man answered. Yes, Rita was his daughter. After identifying herself and expressing her condolences, Maddy asked some general questions, which quickly became more specific. Did he have any idea of how his daughter became acquainted with Reid Temple? No, came his answer. Maddy then probed into his daughter's work at the charity. Was he aware of anything unusual or suspicious related to her time there? Again, no. However, Rita had a close friend who also was employed there, Alison Rosen. Perhaps Maddy should contact her?

After a number of failed attempts, Maddy reached Alison later that evening. Yes, she was a close friend of Rita. Why was Maddy calling? Maddy told her she was a friend of Reid Temple and was looking into the charity's activities. At that point, Alison fell silent for a long stretch until Maddy heard her sigh deeply. Then she heard her mutter. "Maybe I owe it to Rita," she said in a barely audible voice.

"Owe what?" Maddy asked.

"I can't talk now."

"When?"

"I'll be working at the charity tomorrow. If you're there, I might speak to you. But I'll have to be careful."

"Why?"

Ignoring Maddy's question, the woman asked how she would recognize Maddy.

After a moment's thought, Maddy replied that she'd text her a photo of herself.

"Okay," she replied before hanging up.

Snaking fingers of moist fog were cresting the peaks of the Santa Cruz mountains on Sunday when Maddy hopped a BART train to the Stanford University stop and from there, walked the three blocks to the charity. Soon she was standing in front of a pea-green, art-deco-styled building where out front, a large group of people were milling around. Above the gathered crowd a banner had been hung that said "Relief From Hunger Foundation. Charity Bazaar today,"

Once inside, Maddy was immediately set upon by a spotty young man clutching a sheaf of colored paper in his left hand.

"Raffle ticket lady?"

"No thanks, I'm here to see some--"

"It's for charity," he said, persisting. "And it's a great prize. A new smartphone."

Maddy shrugged. "How much?"

"Five bucks. How many you want?"

"Just one."

After taking her money and scratching her name on one of the tickets, he shoved it into her hand. "Good luck lady."

Stuffing the ticket in her coat pocket, Maddy began to make her way through the surging mass of people circulating through the building. Against the wall to her left, was a table stacked with pamphlets explaining the charity's mission and detailing its efforts at feeding the world's poor. Just beyond, in a courtyard visible through a set of double doors a row of tents was visible, where items donated by supporters of the organization were being auctioned to the highest bidder. And in the center of the room, a group of people milled noisily around a stage where an emcee with a microphone was addressing the crowd through a PA system that threatened to drown out all conversation. After a minute or two of walking around the room, Maddy heard someone call her name. Turning, she saw a woman about 35, with freckles and prematurely grey hair yanked into a ponytail, peering out from behind a partition. She was waving for Maddy to come closer.

At that precise moment, a voice boomed over the PA system and echoed through the room:

"Ladies and gentlemen," a man shouted from the podium in the center of the room. "We have a celebrity in our midst today." Then pointing in Maddy's direction, he said "It's Maddy Daniel, anchorwoman of the GBS news!" In a flash, all heads turned toward

Maddy and a shower of enthusiastic applause filled the air. Feeling her face flash white hot, Maddy, after muttering 'God no,' beneath her breath, smiled and gamely waved to the crowd.

When the applause subsided, the man started again. "It's wonderful having Ms. Daniel with us today supporting such a worthy cause. And I'm sure everyone here would be delighted if she would agree to say a few words to us. Would everyone like that?"

A roar spiraled up from the crowd. Maddy, in an attempt to beg off, smiled wanly and with a wave of her hand, tried to shush the crowd. But when the man wouldn't relent, Maddy turned to flash an expression of helplessness at the woman who'd just been calling to her, but saw that she had disappeared. Perplexed, Maddy scanned the room hoping to spot her, but she was gone. Then, with a groan, she started toward the stage.

She'd just reached the steps to the podium when she felt someone tugging at her sleeve. Turning, she saw it was the kid that had sold her the raffle ticket minutes earlier. He was shouting something that she'd couldn't discern over the crowd noise. Turning in his direction, she shook her head and pointed to her ears.

"Lady," he yelled, his words cutting through like radio signals penetrating static, "you won the raffle! Go over there to claim your prize." He was pointing to tables that lined the wall to her left.

Nodding, Maddy mouthed a thank you and made her way up the steps to the stage where she was greeted with enthusiastic applause.

After spending a few minutes placating the gathering with platitudes over the importance of charity work, Maddy left the podium and again scanned the crowd for the woman she'd just met. After minutes of futile searching, she reluctantly made her way to the area where she would claim her prize. While waiting to be served, she noticed that the table was stacked with books. Looking closely, she realized that every book was the same: "Dreams of a New Palestine" by Sahn Rameer.

Noticing her gaze, the charity worker spoke. "That's a wonderful book," she said. "The world would be a much better place if everyone thought like he did."

"Why are they here?"

"Don't you know?"

"Know what?"

"Mr. Rameer is our primary benefactor. He's a wonderful man."

Startled at this revelation, Maddy hesitated a moment, then handed the woman her raffle ticket. "I guess I won," she said.

Wordlessly, the woman took the ticket from her hand. As she peered at it to ensure it was the winning stub, Maddy suddenly became aware of a tapping sound coming from her right. Turning, she saw a blind man in a Fedora wearing midnight blank lenses and wielding a red-tipped cane, approach with halting steps and stop approximately three feet from where she was standing. Reacting to the sound from the man's cane, the woman behind the table looked up and seeing the blind man, flinched noticeably. After pausing for a long moment, she reached hesitantly toward a stack of smartphones positioned to her left. Then after glancing warily at the blind man once more, she slowly withdrew the phone that was positioned second from the top and with a trembling hand, passed it to Maddy.

After murmuring thanks, Maddy's cell phone vibrated. Checking, she saw that she'd received a text message from Alison. "Meet me at the café just south of here in fifteen minutes," it read. After spending a couple of minutes leafing through a display copy of Rameer's book, Maddy left the charity and headed for the café, which, with the exception of an Asian couple huddled in a corner, was empty.

After seating herself and ordering ice tea, Maddy began to peruse the menu. Soon, her concentration was interrupted by a tap, tap tapping on the wooden floor of the restaurant. Looking up, she saw that the blind man she'd seen earlier at the charity was slowly making his way into the restaurant. After bumping into first a pillar, then a chair, a waiter hustled over and carefully guided him to a table maybe twenty feet from where she sat.

Soon the waiter approached to take Maddy's order. Opening her menu, she was about to ask him a question when she heard a commotion coming from her right. Turning, she saw that the blind man had jumped from his chair, and with his cane clattering loudly to the floor behind him, was dashing straight for her. Just as he reached her, he stooped low for something, then broke for the door, zig-zagging crazily at the last second to avoid a couple just entering. Then with Maddy's new smartphone clutched tightly in his right hand, he bolted through the door and dashed from the restaurant.

Chapter 19

Struggling to make sense of what had just taken place, Maddy sat blankly, her unfocused eyes staring out the restaurant window. A minute later, a woman approached whom Maddy recognized as Alison, making her way toward the café. Then, just as she reached the front door, a man with protruding ears and wearing a multi-colored Panama hat raced up, said a few words to her, then pushed a satchel into her arms. Gripping the parcel, she joined Maddy at her table and introduced herself.

"Who was that man?" Maddy asked.

"I've never seen him before," Alison said. "Apparently he works for the charity in some capacity."

Noticing that Maddy was staring at the satchel, Alison told her it was proceeds from the charity bazaar.

"I have to deliver them to our accountants," she said. "And apparently they need them right now. It's not far from here," she said, eyeing the satchel. "Do you mind if we walk? We can talk on the way."

Soon the two women were heading at a brisk pace in a southerly direction. Maddy asked why Alison didn't speak to her inside the charity. I can't be seen talking to you, she replied. Maddy asked why.

"Because I know things. Rita knew things too and look what happened to her."

Maddy asked if she was afraid for her safety. Before she replied, Alison asked Maddy why she was in Palo Alto.

"I think there might be a connection," Maddy replied, "between the charity and--"

"Reid Temple's death?"

Maddy, startled, stared back at Alison. "How did you—"

"As I said," Alison said, cutting her off, "I know things."

Maddy asked if she was close with Rita. Best friends, came her reply.

"Reid didn't kill her."

"No kidding." Alison replied.

"Well," Maddy said, "why was she murdered?"

"I already told you. She knew things. Strange going's on. With Metrius, the Metrius Foundation ---"

"Metrius?" Maddy, replied shocked. "What does the charity have to do with Metrius?"

"Would Reid Temple have flown all the way to Northern California if there wasn't a connection?" Alison asked. She explained that The Relief From Hunger Foundation was supported by the Metrius Endowment. She worked for Barry International and Rita Sessions worked for Rameer Electronics. When the Metrius Endowment was announced, all employees were strongly encouraged to donate time to the charity. It was almost a job requirement. That's how she and Rita had met. Anyway, the charity had been around forever. For years it was solely Littleton Barry's baby, used for charitable work and as a tax write off. When he and

Rameer teamed up to develop Metrius, Barry pushed Rameer to get directly involved, probably to rehabilitate his public image, which had been tainted by some radical views he'd espoused when he was younger.

Maddy asked her why Reid had met with Rita.

"She was the facilities manager for Rameer Electronics. She starting discovering things she probably shouldn't have."

"Like what?"

"Like employees disappearing, only to turn up later at a secret facility."

"A secret facility? Where?"

"In a remote part of the California desert."

"The desert!" Maddy exclaimed. "Why that explains--"

"Exactly. What Reid was doing there."

"What goes on there?"

"No one knows. I assume that's why Reid and Rita met. All I know is that it's under heavy security and anyone who tries to get near it better have their life insurance paid up. As Reid's death obviously makes clear."

"Whatever's going on there," Maddy said, "it's important enough to kill people over." With her mind spinning from what she'd learned, Maddy and Alison resumed their trek toward their destination. After a silent minute, Maddy spoke.

"I've just learned that Reid and Rita didn't dine alone that night. There was a second man."

"A second man? That's news to me."

"It's the best lead I have at this point. He was there for an hour or so before departing. Apparently he was in his 40's, dark complexion, strong build and an unruly beard. Does that ring any bells?"

Alison thought for a moment, then shook her head.

"There's something else," Maddy said. "Earlier, I won a raffle for a smartphone. When I was at the café, a blind man, or someone pretending to be blind, stole the phone from my purse and dashed out the door. Any idea why?"

Shaking her head again, she said no.

"What else can you tell me about the charity?"

"Lots of weird things happening there over the past year," Alison replied. "Shady characters hanging around. Threats against volunteers who ask too many questions. One day when I was doing some filing, a couple of rough looking characters got very angry with me. They probably figured I was snooping, but I wasn't. But the way they reacted freaked me out. Anyway, I got out of there as fast as I could, but I was scared."

Maddy shook her head. "I'm completely in the dark on a key point. How are the deaths of Reid and Rita related to the charity? And to the secret facility?"

"Well, the answer to that obviously lies with what's going on there. Figure that out and you'll have your answer."

"Did Rita ever talk to you about being afraid for her life?"

"Never. That is, not until two weeks ago. Then she said something to me that was very strange. She told me that if anything should happen to her, she'd know who was responsible."

"Did she tell you who it was?" Maddy asked.

Alison hesitated. "Yes. At the time I thought she being paranoid. But now---"

"Will you tell me who it is?"

"You're a reporter, not a policeman. I think I should talk to them first."

"Won't you please tell me?" Maddy asked, a pleading in her voice.

"I don't know Maddy, I---". At that moment, Alison glanced down at the satchel in her hand, then eased Maddy to a halt. "Here we are."

They'd stopped in front of a dilapidated house with a sagging roof and a patchwork of broken windows. Puzzled, Alison checked the address above the front door, then turned toward her Maddy with a look of bewilderment.

"I don't get it," she said. "This is where I'm supposed to drop the receipts off, but it appears to be deserted."

"Are you sure you've got the address right?" Maddy asked.

"It's right here on the satchel."

"Hmm." Maddy stared at the note on the briefcase, then scanned the area for a moment before turning back to Alison. "I'll walk down a couple of houses. Maybe I'll run into someone who knows the area."

Maddy had walked a short distance when she heard Alison call her name. "I've decided to tell you who it was Rita suspected," she said waving Maddy back. "You deserve to know. It was-"

At that moment, the satchel in Alison's hand exploded, slicing the air with her body parts and blood and sending Maddy, screaming and tumbling violently backward. A flash second later, something jagged and sharp powered into her chest.

Chapter 20

Minutes before the bomb exploded that killed Alison, an aide burst into the Washington D.C. office of George Shuba, Secretary of Homeland Security for the United States and handed him a communique. After skimming the note, Shuba spat out an epithet and reached for his phone.

"Set up a video conference with France's Minister of Security and the head of the MI5 in Great Britain to begin in one hour," he barked into the phone. The aide on the other end of the line protested, saying it was late in Europe and they would likely be asleep.

"Then get their asses out of bed. And while you're at it, get the heads of all U.S. security agencies and the NRC down here too." After hanging up the phone, his eyes flashed back to the memo. "I don't believe it," he muttered. "Level Red….a goddam Level Red alert."

An hour later, he was sitting at a conference table surrounded by representatives from the National Security Administration, the CIA, the Pentagon and the Nuclear Regulatory Commission. On the conference line were his counterparts in Great Britain and Europe. After staring hard at the communique in his hand, Shuba addressed them in a solemn voice.

"Ladies and gentlemen, this communique was received by the *Al Jadeera* news service in New York and forwarded to me a little over an hour ago," he said. "As you can see, it contains a severe threat against our three countries." After asking if anyone were familiar with the sect that issued the communique and getting no affirmative replies, he continued.   "I'm directing our National Terrorism Advisory System to issue an Imminent Threat Alert for the United States. It's imperative that you do the same for your countries."

At that point, Ian Dunlop, the head of Britain's MI5 security service, spoke up. "How do we know this group can do what they claim ?" he asked.

"We don't," Shuba said, "but until we find out, we can't afford to provoke them. If we're wrong, the outcome is too terrible to contemplate."

When France's head of security raised the issue of evacuations, a black silence descended over the room.

Shuba finally spoke. "Evacuations may be necessary. But in my view, any talk of that is premature at this point."

When the meeting ended forty minutes later, Shuba turned to a deputy. "Get the guys responsible for this thing…what's it called, Metrius? Get these assholes on a plane to Washington immediately. I want them in front of a closed-door Senate committee. We need to find out if this threat is real and if so, how in hell it happened."

After the group dispersed, Shuba again reached for the communique and with acid searing the back of his throat, re-read its contents. He skipped over the first half in which the authors of the message expressed solidarity with Muslims throughout the world. It was the second half that he found the most chilling:

To the governments of the United States, Great Britain, France and all peoples of the world: We have infected all deployments of the Metrius nuclear energy technology with an undetectable virus. As a result, capabilities encoded with the virus enable us to remotely trigger events that will result in detonation of all Metrius-enabled reactors thirty days from the issuing of this communique unless our conditions are met.

Shuba skimmed over the list of conditions: a lifting of all economic sanctions by Western-aligned nations against all Middle Eastern states, the liberation of Palestine from Israeli occupation and the establishment of a Palestinian homeland. Lastly the group demanded that Israel relinquish all lands taken during the 1967 Middle East war.

And if the conditions were not met? Shuba's eyes flashed to the dire warnings contained in the missive's final paragraph:

Any effort to stop us is futile. The virus we have encoded in the Metrius software enables us to control all processes related to the nuclear plants, including the control of valves, switches and security systems. As a result:

- *Any attempt to detect and remove the virus from any or all of the plants will immediately be detected and will result in immediate detonation of all three plants.*

- *Any attempt to shut the plants down will immediately be detected and will result in the immediate detonation of all three plants, disbursement of nuclear fallout over three countries, the deaths of millions of people and hundreds of miles of land in the US and Europe rendered permanently uninhabitable.*

You have until August 14th, 8 p.m. Eastern Daylight Time.

حر فلسطين إلى

--The Fourth Order

Chapter 21

Lying on the pavement covered in blood and debris, Maddy, stunned by the percussive power of the explosion, moaned. With a trembling hand, she reached for her left leg, where a piece of shrapnel had ripped into her calf, leaving a gaping wound that pooled blood to the pavement. Sensing a painful area just above her left breast, she reached up to massage it and felt the outline of Reid's amulet in her blouse pocket. Reid's keepsake, something she'd promised him she'd always carry, had stopped shrapnel from tearing into her chest, possibly killing her.

Through half-focused eyes, Maddy became aware of strange faces looming over her.

"Are you alright?" she heard a man ask.

Easing herself to a sitting position, Maddy felt something warm dripping into her right eye. Reaching up, she realized that her head was cut deeply just below her scalp line. "I was just standing there, when….I think I'm ok."

"You'd better come with us," the man said. "We can get you to a hospital."

Maddy, trying to focus, shook her head. "I need to tell the police what happened. Oh my God, poor Alison."

The man persisted, slipping his hands beneath her right arm in an attempt to lift her to her feet.

As Maddy pulled away, she felt something hard shoved into her ribs, a revolver. "Co-operate or you're dead," said the man.

The wail of a police siren cut the air. In a flash, the man broke for a late model SUV that was idling at the curb and raced from the scene.

When the police arrived, they immediately summoned paramedics to take Maddy to an emergency clinic where, after refusing a pair of crutches, she was treated for her injuries. Ninety minutes later, she was taken to Palo Alto police headquarters where a police sergeant questioned her extensively about the day's events. When asked why she was at the charity, Maddy told them she was following a story.

"What story?"

"The murder of Reid Temple," she replied.

The police sergeant snorted dismissively. Didn't she mean his suicide?

Maddy, exhausted and impatient, spat out a curse. "I'll tell you what," she said, glaring at him. "Send some of Palo Alto's finest down to the Southern California desert where Reid's body was found and see what you find. And while you're at it, check the charity and find the guy who gave us the bomb." She then repeated the story that Alison had told her about the secret facility.

Maddy spent the better part of an hour skimming through mugshots in the hope of finding the man who gave Alison the satchel or the person who'd attempted to kidnap her. After a fruitless fifty minutes, the police transported Maddy back to her hotel. That night, after picking with disinterest at a room service meal, she fell into bed injured, exhausted and demoralized.

Chapter 22

On Monday, Maddy was awakened early by the throbbing of her injured leg. After limping into the kitchenette to brew some coffee, she switched on the television and like the rest of the nation, was stunned to learn of the plot against the Metrius reactors. After digesting every bit of information she could on the crisis, she switched around until she found a local news program reporting on the charity bombing. She was relieved to find that her name was not mentioned by the reporter covering the story.

Maddy's mind flashed back to the mysterious man who joined Reid and Rita in the restaurant before Rita was murdered. Would identifying him provide a clue to their deaths? Maddy, battling a rising sense of hopeless at solving the murder of the man she now realized she loved, was determined to find out. But now, with her bereavement leave coming to an end, she had to return to Los Angeles.

Arriving at the San Jose airport at 10 am, Maddy was immediately thrust into an environment of chaos and confusion. The threat against the Metrius plants had triggered a nationwide security alert and burly National Guardsmen armed with semi-automatic weapons stalked the airport. Lines of travelers waiting to board their flights snaked from overloaded security checkpoints into the terminal, clogging airport walkways. All the while, televisions throughout the facility blared a constant series of increasingly shrill special reports, further rattling the already nervous people clustered around them.

Maddy, after stopping at her doctor's office to have her wounds redressed, arrived at work to find Ed Snider, Pete Martin, Ashley Stevens, Mako and the entire news team on a conference call with network brass in New York. As she limped into the room, Snider, who was effusively agreeing with everything being said by the GBS New York news director, scowled in her direction. When the meeting ended, Snider waved Maddy over. Ten minutes later, Maddy hobbled into her office and slammed the door. Mako joined her a minute later, her face a mask of concern.

"God Maddy, what happened to you?"

Maddy quickly updated her on the tumultuous events of Sunday. When the story was complete, Mako sat in stunned silence, as if disbelieving what she had heard. "Jeez, you were almost killed. And that poor woman from the charity. What's it all about?"

Maddy groaned. "I wish I knew. We've got a terrorist plot against Metrius that's paralyzing three countries, a secret facility in a remote desert area doing who knows what and three murders. Not to mention a charity that's somehow at the center of it all."

"What's up with the blind guy and your stolen smartphone?" Mako asked. "How's that involved with all this?"

"No idea."

"Did you tell the police about the secret facility?"

"Yes. They're checking it out."

Mako, her mind flashing back to the meeting, smiled at Maddy. "I couldn't believe the look on Snider's face when the bigshots in New York told him they wanted you to handle all the stories involving the threat against Metrius. That must've teed him off."

"Well, " Maddy replied dryly, "that's not going to happen. When the meeting was over, Ed called me over. It seems that his view of my role in this crisis is different than New York's. He wants me to stay out of it."

Mako reacted with shock. "Stay out of it? Is he kidding? You're at the center of it."

"Snider wants Pete to handle the big Metrius stories. All of them."

"Wait a sec," Mako said, throwing her hands in the air. "He can't get away with that. New York calls the tune. If they want you on the story, he'll have to comply."

"Oh, New York will see me all right," Maddy replied with a roll of her eyes. "But my role with be strictly cosmetic. Snider's assigning me all the background stuff, like features on previous terrorist threats, the history of discord in the Middle East, but all the breaking news belong to Pete." Maddy, exhaling heavily, fixed Mako with a baleful stare. "You know what he said to me? Viewers want men to handle the big stories! Can you believe that shit?"

Mako suddenly remembered something. "I finally heard from Professor Buchar."

"Who?"

"The professor from Santa Cruz. You know, the guy my father knew who worked on Metrius."

Maddy recalling, nodded.

"As it turns out, he's in Los Angeles and can meet with us Friday evening. It could lead to something. Apparently, he was involved in some way with Metrius security. If anyone has inside dope on what's going on, it could be him."

"What's he doing in LA?"

"A seminar or something," Mako said. "From what I gather from my father, this guy's quite a character."

"In what way?" Maddy asked.

"Just a bit off-beat," Mako replied. "I guess we'll find out soon enough."

Maddy glanced at her watch. "Almost time for my newscast," she told Mako. "I'll see you in the studio."

Maddy hastily reviewed her news copy, then after a stop in the makeup department, slowly made her way down the dimly-lighted corridor to the studio. With her mind still on the events of the past two days, she navigated trance-like through a tangle of camera cables until she reached the anchor desk and sat down next to Pete Martin, who grunted a brusque hello. After a microphone was placed around her neck, she watched as Mako held up five fingers, then one-by-one counted them down until finally the bright red tally light atop the camera burst to life. "Good evening, Los Angeles," she heard herself say. "Tonight, three countries brace for the worst as a radical group threatens the world with nuclear terror." Then, swallowing hard, Maddy continued. "For the latest on this breaking story, here's Pete Martin."

Following her newscast, Maddy was just about to leave work when her phone rang. When she answered, she was greeted by a male voice that was barely audible over the roar of background traffic.

"Maddy Daniel?"

"Who's this?"

"No names. Not yet anyway."

"What do you want?"

"I have information on Reid Temple."

"Did you know Reid?"

"We had dinner once." A siren blared in the background.

"When?"

"The night Rita Sessions was killed."

Stunned, Maddy dropped her briefcase to her desktop. "You were with Reid and Rita that night?"

"Yes."

"How do I know this isn't a prank?"

"You want proof?"

"Yes."

"Scars."

"What?"

"Scars. On his hands. Fresh ones."

Maddy thought back to the injuries Reid sustained trying to save the sick bird.

"Tell me your name."

"Meet me."

"Where?"

"You know Larchmont Village?"

Maddy recalling the commercial district in central Hollywood, said she did.

"Just south of the hardware shop on Larchmont Avenue is an abandoned storefront that sits back off the street. Meet me there tomorrow morning at 10 am. Then I'll tell you what I know." With a sharp snap, the caller hung up.

The following morning, Maddy was on Larchmont Avenue, impatiently standing before a storefront with windowpanes that reflected an empty void. She shot a glance at the bank clock across the street. 10:20. With her weight on the heel of her good leg, she stared blankly at the pavement, thoughts clicking through her head like a turnstile. Where was this guy? His description of the scars on Reid's arms made it clear he'd seen him, so why hadn't he shown up? With a rising sense of frustration, she checked her watch. Five more minutes, she thought. A half-hour later she gave up and headed back to her car. During the drive to work, Maddy, thinking of the events of the weekend and the evolving connection to Metrius, resolved to contact Littleton Barry to share what she'd learned. When she rang his office later that day, she instead was connected to Jason DeMir.

"Jason, I need to see Littleton," she told him.

"'Sorry Maddy, but he and Sahn were called to Washington yesterday," he said. "They're being grilled by Congress over the Metrius crisis. The country's in a tizzy over all this and it's all for nothing."

"How can a terrorist threat against nuclear reactors be nothing?"

"Littleton, Sahn and the development team poured over the security procedures that were in place during the Metrius development period. Everything was airtight. The found no evidence of any tampering with Metrius. They're in Washington now telling that to a Senate committee."

"The software may be okay," Maddy replied, "but there's a problem." She then told Jason what she'd learned of the charity, its relationship to the Metrius Foundation and of course, the attack on her and Alison.

"Jeez Maddy, I had no—" Then, with his voice rising, he abruptly switched gears. "Quick Maddy!" he shouted. "Turn on your TV!"

Flipping on her office monitor, Maddy saw that a special report was being aired from the U.S. State Department. Standing in the blinding glare of television lights, George Shuba, flanked by the heads of all U.S. security agencies, was reading a statement. And standing just behind him were Littleton Barry and Sahn Rameer. Ratcheting up the volume on her television, Maddy listened intently as he spoke.

"The government of the United States, Great Britain and France, in conjunction with the State of Israel, will not comply with demands from the radical group calling itself The Fourth Order. Further, after extensive consultation with the developers of the Metrius energy source, we have determined that claims by this sect that they control plant operations are baseless. The co-developers of this

revolutionary technology, Littleton Barry and Sahn Rameer, who are with me today, assure me that the Metrius technology was developed under the most stringent security conditions and that claims that the technology is infected with a malevolent computer virus are unfounded.

The governments of the U.S., Britain and France reject terrorism in all of its forms and will not negotiate with extremists. To residents of the U.S., England and France living in the vicinity of a Metrius reactor, we say to you: there is no danger. And to members of the radical sect calling themselves The Fourth Order, we say this: you cannot escape justice. We will track you down wherever you hide."

At 8:20 pm that evening, residents living near Indian Point in Poughkeepsie New York heard an explosion. Minutes later, RadNet, the EPA air monitoring system that samples air in the upstate New York area flashed an alert to the U.S. Nuclear Emergency Tracking Center in Washington D.C.: dangerous levels of radiation were spewing over Poughkeepsie. The source: the Indian Point nuclear power reactor.

Chapter 23

Wednesday, July 19th 9:20 pm EDT

The White House, Washington D.C.

Less than an hour after the Poughkeepsie radiation leak was detected, White House operators patched through a call from President William Loes to George Shuba at his offices at National Security Headquarters. In the room with Shuba, or on a conference line, were the heads of all U.S. security agencies.

"Dammit George," Loes spat into the phone, "just hours ago, people on three continents heard you say there was nothing to worry about. What happened?"

"Mr. President, we've obviously underestimated the capability of this group."

"And overestimated the intelligence of these guys who created this mess."

"They assured me Mr. President that---"

"I don't give a fuck what they told you."

"Yes, Mr. President."

The line fell silent. Drumming his fingers nervously, Shuba waited for Loes to continue.

"In the meantime, we have no choice but to prepare for the worst," the president said. "George, convene a team of the country's top physicists, meteorologists, computer modelers and health specialists. Anybody with expertise in airborne hazards and go to work."

Uncertain, Shuba spoke up. "On what, Mr. President?"

"God dammit George, we need to set up an evacuation zone around the plant in case it completely detonates. But first I want answers. How much radiation will be released into the air if the plant explodes? How many will die immediately? What are the long term effects related to cancers and deformities? And what are the chances of containing the radiation? Once I have that information, I'll know how large the evacuation zone must be." The president exhaled deeply. "Now, let's focus on our immediate problem. We have a cloud of radiation spreading over upstate New York and haven't much time to decide on a course of action. I want to hear from the folks in the room. What are your recommendations?"

Shuba spoke first. "Mr. President, our first action must be to alert residents of New York of the danger. And we've got to do it now."

Shaking his head, James Lonborg, director of the NSA, spoke up. "I disagree," he said firmly. "Our first priority is to ensure we don't have a panic on our hands. We need to get the Army and National Guard deployed. Only then should we issue a general alert."

Shuba scoffed. "That could take hours," he said, fixing Lonborg with a stare. "What about the residents of Poughkeepsie? Don't we alert them or are they just collateral damage?"

"Of course we warn them," Lonborg shot back. "But only after the Army and National Guard arrive. Otherwise, we'll have chaos on our hands."

"Do you realize how many people will die as a result?" Shuba replied, growing agitated. "Every minute we delay will cost us lives."

"And how many will die sitting on clogged roadways and in overloaded airport terminals?" Lonborg replied. "I tell you, we have no choice." Around the table, heads began to nod in agreement.

The president spoke. "Ok, here's my decision. First we mobilize the Army and the Guard. Once they're in place, we issue a general alert."

Alarmed at what he heard, John Logan, deputy secretary of the U.S. Nuclear Regulatory Commission, spoke up. "I respectfully disagree, Mr. President," he said. "It'll be hours before the Army and National Guard get there. By then, thousands, possibly millions will be exposed to lethal doses of radiation."

The head of the FBI spoke next. "Mr. President," he said, "if word gets out that we delayed alerting the American people, there will be political consequences."

"The politics be damned," Loes snapped. "The radiation leak concerns me, but a nation-wide panic will only make things worse. We have no choice but to wait until the Guard and the Army are in place. Is everyone in agreement?" Around the table, a grudging acceptance of reality was settling in. "Yes, Mr. President," Shuba replied.

Reacting quickly, John Logan excused himself and left the room. After making sure he wasn't observed, he ducked into a doorway and pulled out his phone.

"Honey, listen very carefully." Logan said to his wife when she answered. "and do exactly as I say. Get the kids out of bed and get the hell out of Poughkeepsie. And do it this minute."

"What's going--"

"No time to explain, just do it! Do it now!"

His next call was to the head of the Washington bureau of NBC News.

Within minutes, news of the radiation leak broke and flashed around the world.

Chapter 24

Poughkeepsie, New York, Thursday, July 20th

"You a prayin' man?"

The question was posed by the driver of a large transit bus snarled in rush hour traffic to a man in a business suit seated directly behind him.

"No."

"Well, if what they're sayin' on the radio is true," the driver said, slamming his brakes and bringing his bus to a shuddering halt, "it might be a good time to start." With that, the driver bolted from his seat and dashed from the bus, leaving his vehicle idling in the middle of a crowded intersection.

In Poughkeepsie, word of the radiation leak hit like a drone strike, transforming the city into a freak, alternate world of chaos and panic.

Upon hearing the news, bank manager Angie Boyer lurched from her desk and raced for her car. Minutes later, swerving to miss a pedestrian, she roared into the parking lot of Grant elementary school and exited her car at a dead run. Bursting through the doors of the administration office, she encountered a throng of distraught parents, all demanding access to their children. Standing at the front of the group and desperately trying to calm them was the school principal.

"We have orders from the governor," he yelled, straining to be heard over shouts from the group. "The National Guard is on its way and will oversee evacuations. Until they arrive, all children are being kept in the cafeteria and none will be released." Enraged at his words, a man in an expensive three piece suit standing nearby threw a punch that sent the principal, bleeding and dazed, crashing to the floor. Spitting out a curse, Boyer bolted from the office and ran full speed for the cafeteria where she spotted her daughter. She was immediately confronted by a female vice-principal. "No children are to be released until--." At that point, a crashing blow from Boyer's right hand sent the woman sprawling to the floor. Stepping over her prone figure, Boyer grabbed her daughter by the arm and screamed "Let's go!"

Once she had her daughter safely in her car, Boyer stomped the gas pedal and with tires squealing, raced for the parking lot exit. Watching nervously as Boyer's car approached was lanky Derrell Thomas, 58. Working as a security guard hadn't been his dream, but since being laid off from his job as an IT specialist four years earlier, he'd plowed through his savings, and having grown desperate, gratefully accepted the job when it was offered. To his surprise, the work suited him and now, thankful for the opportunity the school district had provided, he was determined not to let them down.

As Boyer's car approached, Thomas stepped forward and nervously raised his hand.

"I'm sorry ma'am," he said as Boyer's car skidded to a halt just inches from where he stood. "But I have orders. No one leaves."

Enraged, Boyer revved her engine menacingly. "Get the hell out of the way," she shouted.

"Please ma'am," Thomas said, his voice rising. "It won't be long until the National Guard arrives."

"I'm warning you!"

"Please—"

Spouting an epithet, Boyer slammed her foot to the floor. In a flash, the car lurched forward, crashing into Thomas and shattering the femurs of both legs. As he was thrown clear, Boyer, with tires screaming, fish-tailed from the lot at high speed, the wild motion of her vehicle sending her careening into an approaching car, instantly killing the occupants of both vehicles.

At a Rite-Aid drug store in East Village, pharmacist Joseph Wilcox, elderly, bespectacled and sporting electronics in each ear, was trying to calm a surging mob demanding access to potassium iodide.

"I'm sorry folks," he yelled, his thin voice barely audible above the shouts of the crowd. "But because of hoarding, we've been ordered to halt sales of potassium iodide until an equitable distribution method is set up. Government orders. I'm asking for your cooperation!"

Reacting, the crowd erupted and began to surge forward. As they did, Ellen Wilkinson, 22 and heavily pregnant, muscled her way to the front of the mob. "My baby, my baby!" she cried out to Wilcox. "I need the pills!" As the plea left her lips, a woman standing to her right, shouted a curse and threw an elbow, sending Wilkinson staggering to the floor. A moment later, someone hurled a bottle of rubbing alcohol at Wilcox, striking him just above the bridge of his nose. Blood pouring from the wound, he made his way to a locked room and with a shaking hand, dialed 911. This is what he heard:

"The 911 system is currently overloaded, Please try again later."

In the Crown Heights section of Poughkeepsie, fifty-two year old Vasile Rakesh, reacting to a chorus of sirens, peered anxiously from the window of his convenience store. According to news reports, looters had been spotted in the area, smashing windows and starting fires. Determined to save his store, he quickly hustled his wife and young daughter to their small apartment out back. After instructing them to lock themselves in, he dashed back to his store. grabbed the baseball bat he'd always kept behind the counter and doused the lights. Then with blood pounding in his ears, he crouched behind the front door and waited. Soon he heard something that sounded like the roar of a car engine, but quickly turned into shouting. Voices boiled up from the tangle, vicious, blood-filled cries of "open up motherfucker!" Peering through the shade, Rakesh saw a mob of young men advancing on his storefront. A flash moment later, a brick smashed against the window, showering Rakesh with broken glass. A young man with tattoos extending from his neck to his arms raised a metal trash can and with a grunt, heaved it at the front door. Absorbing the impact, the door collapsed and the maddened group burst through the opening. Gripping the baseball bat, Rakesh rose to confront them, but a powerful blow sent him sprawling to the floor. After kicking Rakesh in the head, the men stormed through the store, filling their arms with cases of beer and pulling food from racks, while others smashed displays and overturned fixtures. Then with taunting words, they stepped over the prone Rakesh and departed with their spoils.

With blood pouring from his wounds, Rakesh staggered to his feet. Swaying uneasily, he stopped, his eyes taking in the wreckage of his life's work. With his store in shambles, there was nothing to do now but round up his family and get out as quickly as possible. His eyes fell on the grill at the center of the store, one of the few structures left standing. He shook his head. Idiots, he thought. If the news reports were right, the fate of the destructive mob that just left would be no different than the hot dogs that still sizzled there.

In his downtown office, hedge fund manager Jack Harvey eyed his television with growing alarm. Images of highways, choked to a standstill by panicked residents filled the airwaves, making it clear that fleeing Poughkeepsie by car was no longer possible. Hatching a desperate plan, Harvey dashed for his vehicle. As he raced along Glenwood Avenue bound for the train station, Harvey was afforded a first-hand view of the hellish landscape that Poughkeepsie had become: passing a Chevron station, Harvey watched as a young woman, unwilling to wait her turn to fuel her vehicle, knocked an old man to the ground. Passing the local grocery store, Harvey saw an angry mob using a sidewalk bench to batter their way inside. Leading the charge was a man Harvey recognized as a volunteer from the local church.

Arriving at the train station, Harvey encountered a carpet of human madness that spilled from the terminal entrance to the boarding platform. Railroad employees, harriedly trying to stop people from forcing their way aboard already over-packed cars, fought against the surging mob, while conductors signaled frantically to the train's engineer to depart the station. Perched at the edge of the madness were Claudia Beeler and her eighty-five year old mother. Learning of the crisis, she'd hurriedly picked up her mother at the retirement home and raced for the station, hoping to escape to her sisters in Vermont. As the train began to lurch forward, a man standing nearby tripped and fell into Beeler and her mother, sending both women screaming onto the tracks where they were crushed beneath the train's grinding wheels.

Alarmed by the escalating chaos, New York governor John Blanchard declared martial law for Poughkeepsie and the surrounding area at 11 a.m. and by midnight, looters were being shot on sight by Army snipers.

As a wave of terror gripped the eastern United States, a new communique arrived at *al Jardeera* and was quickly flashed to a nervous world:

"The Fourth Order has released a limited amount of radiation into the air surrounding the Poughkeepsie Metrius reactor at Indian Point. Any further questioning of our capabilities will result in even greater destruction. Meet our demands or the plants will be destroyed. You have 25 days."

حر فلسطين إلى

--The Fourth Order

Chapter 25

Thursday July 20th 5:58 pm PDT

That evening, Maddy was on the set of her newscast, eyeing the studio clock with growing anxiety. With just minutes to go before air, there was no sign of her co-anchor. Catching Mako's eye, she mouthed the words "Where's Pete?" Mako, looking anxious, shook her head helplessly.

Finally, at 5:59, the studio door flew open and Pete Martin, with his hair a lazy tangle and weaving noticeably, made his way to the anchor desk and slumped down next to Maddy. Seconds later, Mako queued Maddy. The broadcast had begun.

"Good evening Southern California," viewers heard Maddy say. "In breaking news, a terrorist attack at a New York nuclear reactor triggers a nationwide panic. And now….." Shooting a sidelong glance at her co-anchor, Maddy made a split-second decision. "I have the latest for you."

Watching from his office, Ed Snider exploded with rage. Reaching for his phone, he called the control room. "As soon as this show ends, I'm coming down there," he barked to the news director. "Nobody leaves the set!"

For the next thirty minutes, Snider paced the room, fuming and sputtering. When the broadcast finally concluded, he stalked the length of the hallway to the news set where anxious crew members waited in silence.

"What the fuck is going on here" he shouted, storming his way to the anchor desk. "You," he said, jabbing a finger at Maddy, "were under explicit instructions to let Pete handle the breaking news on the terror threat." As his upbraiding of Maddy continued, Mako struggled to control herself while embarrassed crew members eyed each other uneasily.

Spinning to face the crew. Snider continued. "I want everyone to hear this," he thundered. "This woman," he said pointing again at Maddy, "deliberately disobeyed an order to let Pete…" At that point, Snider turned toward Martin, eyed him for a long moment, then abruptly stopped. Then with a graveyard silence settling over the room, Snider flashed his eyes nervously left and right, then cleared his throat. A moment later he muttered a curt "that will be all" and crew members, whispering between themselves, filed slowly out.

Once everyone was gone, Pete Martin left his spot at the anchor desk and made his way to Snider's side. In hushed tones, he spoke to him for a minute, then after nodding in Maddy's direction once or twice, exited the room. Snider, looking chagrined, stood for a long moment before uneasily approaching Maddy who was still seated in her chair.

"Umm," Snider said haltingly, his arms hanging dead at his sides. After clearing his throat, he started again. "Pete took some pills this morning," Snider said, his eyes fixed on the floor. "Something to do with a cold or something." Finally, in a voice barely audible he said "Ok, that'll be all." Then turning on his heel, he left the studio.

On Friday morning, Maddy received a tip from a source in the LAPD. The body of a Middle Eastern man who had died in a very strange way had been found in a downtown hotel room. Was she interested? After hearing the odd details of the man's death, Maddy grabbed her briefcase and dashed for the door. Forty minutes later, she was standing in front of crime scene investigator on the eighth floor of the Bonaventure Hotel in downtown LA, demanding to see the lead investigator. Soon, a man in a vest with "CSI LAPD" emblazoned on the front, approached.

"I'm Maddy Daniel from GBS news," she said. "I want to see view the body."

"The investigation is ongoing," he replied. "No one gets in."

"Then at least give me some details. What's the cause of death?"

The man shook his head. "We'll make a statement once the investigation is completed. Until then, nothing."

As he spoke, Maddy, straining on her toes to peer into the room, recognized Denis Winters, an investigator with the LA Coroner's office she'd worked with previously. Noticing Maddy, he mouthed the word "Lobby."

Fifteen minutes later, he joined Maddy in a corner of the hotel restaurant. "I can't say much," he said, "but I have a couple of juicy tidbits for you. First of all, the guy was found dead inside of a suitcase."

Maddy scowled. "Sounds like a sex stunt gone wrong."

Winters shook his head. "Nope. The latches to the suitcase were secured from the outside. And there are there no traces of his DNA on the locks or on the outside of the suitcase."

"Weird," Maddy said, puzzled by what she heard. "Any idea of how long he was in there?"

"Not yet."

"Was he alive when he was stuffed in the suitcase."

"We're not sure." He hesitated. "I shouldn't be telling you this, but there's something else." His voice dropped to a whisper. "The guy was completely hairless."

"You mean bald?"

"No, his entire body. Head to toe, not a follicle."

Maddy asked if he'd been ID'd.

"His last name is Darzi," Winters replied. "He appears to be Middle Eastern."

"My contact at the LAPD tells me they found a laptop."

He nodded.

"He also told me that this guy's Internet history showed that he'd been reading up on the three nuclear plants targeted by this terrorist group. Is that true?"

Winters nodded again.

Maddy cocked an eyebrow. "We've got a Middle Eastern guy dead in what appears to be a professional hit. There's info on his computer related to nuclear plants that are under attack. Does that sound fishy?"

"At first, I wasn't sure," he said. "But something happened an hour ago to make me change my mind." Maddy asked him what.

"The Fed's. The FBI and NSA have gotten involved."

Maddy reacted with surprise. "The Feds? What's their role in this?"

"I'm not sure," Winters replied. "But investigators are flying in today. Until they get here we're under orders to keep everything on lockdown."

Maddy's mind worked away at what she'd heard. If security agencies from the federal government were involved, did that mean there was a conclusive link between Darzi's death and the threat against the plants? She had to find out. "When can I view the body?" she asked.

"Sorry Maddy," he replied shaking his head, "not this time. Once the government's involved, my hands are tied."

After thanking him, Maddy returned to work, where she was surprised to find Pete Martin, looking subdued and thoughtful, waiting to see her.

"It's about yesterday," Martin said, sitting down opposite Maddy. "I want to thank you for covering for me." He flashed an uneasy smile. "An incident like that could have destroyed my career. I'm grateful. I really am."

"It was nothing."

"It was big and I'm very thankful." He eyed Maddy, chagrin marking his face. "There's something else." At this point, Martin cleared his throat. "Ed and I have been pretty hard on you. And while I can't speak for him, I just want to tell you how sorry I am.

I've been wrong. I want you to know that if there's anything I can do for you, just ask. I've been at this racket for a long time and well, let's just say, I have a way of getting things done."

Listening to Pete's words, a thought jumped into Maddy's head. "You know," she said, a sly expression marking her face," maybe there is something you can help me with."

Chapter 26

As a crisis mentality gripped the nation, Maddy met Liam Buchar in a downtown Los Angeles hotel room Friday night. For a tenured instructor at a major California university, Buchar had a decidedly non-professorial appearance. Sinewy and lean, with shoulder-length grey-laced hair framing a thin, deeply-lined face, he was clad head to toe in black and sported a pair of gold tipped boots.

As Buchar pulled a beer from the hotel mini-bar, he spoke of his background with Metrius. As a cyber-security expert, he'd been hired as a consultant by Ray Trask during the project's initial months. After reviewing the software and ultimately making a few recommendations, his contract had ended, though he continued consulting on an as-needed basis. Upon learning of the plot against the Metrius plants, he'd used his credentials to once again access the project software in hopes of determining the credibility of the threat. But with the eyes of the world suddenly trained on the deployments, the U.S. government had quickly clamped down on everything and Metrius was now under the tightest security. But before the restrictions took hold, he'd found something troubling; something buried so deeply in the program, he'd nearly missed it. It was a code fragment hidden in the software's least significant bits. Noticing the puzzled look on Maddy's face, he explained that computer source code has building blocks that once added, were never thought of again. Noting her uncomprehending expression, he tried again.

"Think of a girder in a skyscraper," he told her. "Each girder contains dozens of rivets and each building has hundreds of girders. A computer program is similar. Once the foundation is completed, it's quickly overshadowed when the person creating the basic program adds thousands of lines of more significant code on top of it. Bottom line? If somebody decides to dig down far enough into a design and put something there, odds are that no one will ever find it. Which makes it a mother-fucker to detect."

Ignoring his colorful language, Maddy eyed him steadily. "So hard to detect that even the developer can't find it?"

Buchar, mindful of the false assurances issued just days earlier by Littleton Barry and Sahn Rameer shrugged. "The developers of this technology probably reviewed the security procedures they had in place during the development phase and found them to be sufficient. Which explains their misplaced confidence in its safety. But finding something like an embedded virus in program like Metrius, even if you built it, is incredibly difficult. I was lucky. They weren't. It's that simple. And that complicated."

"But I thought Metrius was revolutionary," Maddy said. "How could something like this have happened?"

"Metrius is revolutionary," Buchar continued, "in the way it produces energy. But it's comprised of source code, just like all computer programs. And source code, no matter how sophisticated, can be hacked."

"Any way of telling by whom?" Maddy asked.

"Well, that's the million dollar question, isn't it?" Buchar replied, draining his beer, then puffing his cheeks to stifle a belch. "It's possible the infection came from an outside source. E-mail contains viruses, so maybe someone working on the Metrius project inadvertently introduced it into Metrius by clicking on an infected email. But I doubt it and it's clear its creators do too. It's more likely that someone working for Barry, Reid Temple or Sahn Rameer did it deliberately."

Would he be willing to keep working on the software in the hope he could destroy this virus?

"Funny you should mention that," he replied. "I was contacted by someone from the NSA earlier today. Because of my previous experience with the Metrius software, they want me to work with the government on cracking the virus." He raised his eyes to meet Maddy's. "There was just one problem. I hate the bastards." He got to his feet and moved to the mini-bar for another beer. "I told them to go to hell."

Hearing his words, Maddy was crestfallen. Noting her reaction and thinking of his friendship with Ray Trask, Buchar fell quiet. "Tell you what," he said after a long minute. "I'll call them back tomorrow." He shrugged. "Maybe it won't be too bad."

Grateful, Maddy thanked him and got up to leave. Then remembering, she pulled something from her pocket. "Professor," she said "moments before Ray Trask died, he was trying to send this message to Reid. Reid was convinced Trask had cracked the secret to the Metrius virus and just before he was murdered was trying to convey what he'd learned."

Taking the note, Buchar stared hard at the cryptic words it contained:

Ends just means tri ci

After a long moment, he slowly shook his head, then reached into his pocket for a pen and piece of paper and copied the odd message. "Couldn't hurt to hang onto this," he said stuffing the note into his shirt pocket.

Chapter 27

The following day, Maddy was skimming through her email when something stopped her cold:

My brother was with Reid Temple and Rita Sessions the night she was killed.

--Constant Viewer

Grabbing her cell, Maddy quickly punched in the number shown at the bottom of the email. After a couple of rings, a woman, her voice husky and low, answered.

"Finally," the woman said when she realized who was calling. Maddy asked her name.

"Amber."

"Well Amber," Maddy replied, "You got my attention, but I'm still skeptical of your claim. I need proof."

"You think it's only a coincidence that I've been warning you for weeks of a looming attack on the U.S. and now we have the Metrius crisis?"

Maddy fell silent. "Okay," she said finally, "tell me what you know."

"Not over the phone," she said. "I live in Pasadena. You can be here in less than thirty minutes."

Maddy checked her watch. "Alright," she said, "but I have something to do first. Better give me an hour."

Forty minutes later, Maddy was standing next to the assistant coroner for LA County as he unzipped the body bag on the table in front of him. "Pete said I might be hearing from you," he said as the gruesome form of the body inside was revealed. "But we've got to hurry," he said, his eyes flashing around the room. "This could mean my job."

Scowling at the state of the corpse, Maddy immediately felt nauseous as the overpowering odor of formaldehyde filled the room.

"What he dead or alive when he was put inside the suitcase?"

"Alive," he replied. "The rigor mortis was awful. Think of a human pretzel. It took three of us just to unwind this guy."

"What happened to his hair?"

"My money's on some sort of radiation poisoning. It does that to a person."

"Aside from the twisted limbs, any signs of external bodily injury?" Maddy asked, fighting to quell the queasy feeling in her stomach.

"None."

Maddy asked when the test results would be in.

"Depends on the courts," he said. "An injunction from the federal government arrived this morning. They're suing to move the body to Washington to perform their own autopsy. Until that's settled, nothing happens."

Maddy looked puzzled. "Doesn't state law mandate that a California medical examiner perform the autopsy?"

Yes, he replied, unless there was an overriding national security issue. And apparently, Washington thought there was.

"We're fighting the injunction," he said, "but right now, everything's tied up in legal mumbo-jumbo." After a shrug, he started to close the bag.

At that moment, Maddy spotted something that made her freeze. "Hold it!" she shouted. Pulling a handkerchief from her coat pocket to block the noxious odor emanating from the corpse, she leaned closer and stared at the body's upper right arm through narrowed eyes. What was that oddly shaped scar?

Chapter 28

A half-hour after leaving the coroner's office, Maddy pulled up in front of a small bungalow in north Pasadena and made her way to the front door. Amber, who answered, was a thin, olive-skinned woman in her mid-40's, with a luxurious head of black hair that she wore tucked behind her ears. After turning down an offer of coffee, Maddy scanned the room. Almost immediately, her eyes fell on a collection of ornate statuary nestled inside a bookcase. Noticing, Amber began to speak. She'd been raised in the Middle East, she said. Her mother had died at birth and her father had been killed in the 1987 Palestinian uprising. She'd lived in Hebron in Palestine for most of her life, before entering the United States two years earlier. Maddy listened, wondering what all this had to do with Reid, Rita Sessions and the plot against the Metrius reactors.

A minute later, she found out. Amber had an older brother, she told Maddy. He'd remained in the Middle East, in Tel Aviv, she said. Deeply attached to one another, they'd maintained contact. That is, she said, until eight weeks ago, when he called with a story so strange she doubted its truthfulness.

'He told me he was an agent with the Mossad," Amber said.

"The Israeli secret police that deals with covert operations and counter–intelligence?" Maddy asked.

Amber nodded.

"What was his assignment?" Maddy asked.

"To infiltrate a sect that was suspected of plotting against the Israeli government," Amber replied. "As it turned out, he was successful and had learned of an attack the group was planning. But he was afraid."

"Of what?"

"Of being detected. Then, two weeks later he called to say his worst fears had come to pass."

"He'd been uncovered by the group he'd infiltrated?"

"Yes," Amber replied. "But not before he learned details of their plot. As it turned out, the group was targeting the Metrius plants and not Israel. He also told me that a Northern California charity had been set up as a front for the sect."

Maddy could scarcely believe what she was hearing. If what Amber was saying was true, her brother, the deaths of Reid, Rita Sessions and Alison, the Relief From Hunger Foundation and the plot against the Metrius plants were all connected.

"My brother was convinced his life was endangered," Amber continued "and desperately wanted to escape to the United States. He asked if I would give him a place to stay. That was three weeks ago. Since then," Amber said, despair marking her face, "not a word."

Maddy asked about Reid.

Amber nodded. "Just before he hung up, he told me that he attempted to alert Mr. Temple to the threat against the plants."

"Why not Littleton Barry or Sahn Rameer?"

"Mr. Temple was the only one he could reach."

Maddy asked her why she hadn't she gone to police with her information.

'I'll be deported if I do," Amber replied. "I'm in the country illegally. Anyway, I knew I couldn't relay news like this anonymously. And if I used my name, a background check would be run on me. Unlike the Middle East, journalists in this country have a right to protect their sources. Because of your profession and your connection with Mr. Temple, I wanted to reach you with my story."

Maddy shifted uneasily. If only her lingering nausea would subside, she could think clearly.

Amber, noting Maddy's discomfort, asked her if she was all right.

"Not really," Maddy replied sighing heavily. "I've just come from the LA Coroner's office, where I viewed a body of a man that had been poisoned. It was awful." Maddy then described the gruesome condition of the body and mentioned the odd shaped scar on the inside of the man's right arm.

Hearing Maddy's words, Amber recoiled as if jolted by an electrical current. Yanking up the sleeve of her blouse, she looked at Maddy with a look of incredulity.

"Like this one?" she asked.

Chapter 29

After displaying the scar on her arm to a shocked Maddy, Amber pressed for more information about the body at the coroner's office. After listening to Maddy's description, she began to cry.

"That's Mirit Taham, my brother," she said between sobs. "I know it."

"It can't be," Maddy said. "According to the coroner's office," Maddy replied, "his last name is Darzi."

"I'm sure that's an alias assigned to him by the Israeli government," Amber said, her breath coming in halting spurts now. "Where was he killed?"

"In a downtown Los Angeles hotel room last week," Maddy said, omitting the bizarre details surrounding his death.

"He was here trying to reach me, I'm certain of it," Amber said, composing herself. "But they got to him first," Noting Maddy's confusion, she continued. "Let me explain," she said. "Mirit Taham was my brother. We were born in Palestine. Our mother died during my birth. For the first few years, we were raised by our father. His name was Deron Taham. He was a fanatical Palestinian nationalist, who devoted his life to the destruction of the Israeli state. From the day we were born, he subjected us to a constant stream of propaganda, reciting the evils of the Zionists and how it was our destiny to fight them. He had an odd physical characteristic that was a direct result of his hatred of the Israelis; half of his right ear was missing. I remember asking him about it. He told me that it had been sliced off in a bar fight with an Israeli soldier before I was born. Anyway, one day, when we were very young, he took us to the Qualandia refugee camp where we saw horrible things that happened to the people who lived there. Later that day – I remember it like it was yesterday though it was over thirty-five years ago – he took us to a hidden room in our house –a room that neither my brother or myself had known existed -- and dipped a red-hot metal iron with a flattened top into an urn containing ashes of some sort. He then burned it into our arms."

Maddy grimaced. "How awful."

"It was. Because of my father's anger and volatility, I lived in a state of constant fear. My only friend and protector was Mirit, who did everything he could to shelter me from the horror we experienced. Anyway, not long after, teachers at our school, seeing the burn marks, summoned school officials and after some legal wrangling, we were removed from us our father's custody by child protection services. From there, we were placed into foster homes."

"What was the significance of the scar?"

"I'm not sure. But my brother and I had seen it before." Amber slowly shook her head. "There were always strange men around my father. And every one of them had the identical scar on their arm. And guns, always lots of guns around. On certain nights of the week, we were locked away for hours. If we protested, we were beaten. Shortly after being confined to our rooms, we'd hear sounds of people arriving at our house, followed by hours of strange noises and chanting. I assume they gathered in the secret room my father revealed to us that day. What their purpose was, I don't know."

"What happened after you were removed from his custody?"

"We bounced around from one foster home to another before finally settling in one that kept us until we were sixteen. Following that, I remained in the Middle East for fifteen years before finally coming to this country."

"Did you remain in contact with Mirit?"

"Constantly. I loved him. In the darkest hours of my childhood, he watched over me. Even now, I think of him as my protector."

"And your father?" Maddy asked.

"Killed in the 1987 Palestinian uprising."

"Did he attempt to contact you after you were removed from his custody?"

"Many times. But as I grew older, I realized what he'd done to us. It's odd," Amber continued, reflecting, "but for years, my father tried to teach me to hate. 'Hate will keep you alive' he told me on many occasions. Hatred for the Israeli's, hatred for infidels, hatred for everyone except the Palestinians. When I was removed from his madness, I came to see just how destructive hatred can be. Today, thanks to a lot of hard work, I hate only one person: my father."

"How did your brother end up as an agent for the Mossad?"

"I don't know. As I say, he kept all of that from me. Like me, he was extremely bitter over our father's treatment of us. I can only surmise that he was determined to totally reject his thinking. How better to do that than fight on behalf of Israel?"

"And being of Palestinian descent," Maddy said, "would made it easier to infiltrate radical groups that might be plotting against the government."

Amber nodded. "Which probably led him to the group targeting the Metrius plants."

Maddy, realizing the government involvement would make it impossible for Amber to view the body at the morgue, asked if she would be willing to view a snapshot to confirm his identity. She said yes. After thanking her, Maddy said goodbye.

Outside, the sun had sunk below the trees throwing shadows the length of the street. Once in her car, Maddy sat staring out the window, her mind on Amber's story. It was now clear that Reid, having learned of the threat against Metrius and the charity's shady role in it, had met with Amber's brother and Rita Sessions in Palo Alto to get as much information on the plot as he could. Something else was evident: the man who contacted her saying he was at the restaurant that night was Amber's brother, who was cut down sometime between his call and their scheduled meeting. The message was clear: the Fourth Order had inside information. Everyone who'd tried to foil the plot against Metrius…Reid, Rita, Ray Trask, Amber's brother and Alison were now dead.

Feeling a sudden chill. Maddy hurriedly snapped the locks on her car. The low rumble of a car starting behind her made her jump. Suddenly edgy, she scanned the length of the street through narrowed eyes. Seeing nothing, she started her car and headed back to work. But with each mile she drove, she gripped her cell phone tightly and had her eyes fixed on the rear view mirror.

Chapter 30

July 31st

For Liam Buchar it was hell realized. As a lifelong hater of government, agreeing to work with the National Security Agency was odious enough. The real kicker came when he learned that until the Metrius bug was cracked, he'd be housed in a 'skiff' --NSA shorthand for a Sensitive Compartmented Information Facility in downtown Los Angeles where, with just two weeks left before the plants would detonate, a last-ditch effort would be made to disable the Metrius virus. As a non-government worker, Buchar would be confined to the facility 24/7 and subjected to constant oversight to ensure that classified material unrelated to Metrius could not be compromised. The bottom line? Once there, he couldn't leave. And to ensure compliance, Iris Recognition scanners were mounted at every exit, making escape for anyone without the proper authorization impossible. And in Buchar's area, the only ones with that freedom were Irv Noren, a bullet-headed NSA supervisor with a carnival mirror body and one or two of his lieutenants.

Upon his arrival, Buchar, was introduced to members of the emergency response team. The group, comprised of computer experts from Homeland Security, had been instrumental in cracking the infamous Stuxnet computer virus that crippled computers in seven countries in 2010. Also arriving at the same time as Buchar were elite members from security agencies in Britain and France, having been enlisted by the NSA to aid in the effort. After being shown to his cubicle, Buchar, to his disgust, was herded into a conference room for an orientation meeting.

"For the first time in human history," Irv Noren announced once the new arrivals were seated. "the world is being threatened by the specter of nuclear terrorism." After taking a minute to eyeball the faces in the room, he continued. "I don't feel it necessary to remind you of the challenge we face or the limited amount of time we have to prevent this crisis. But before we resume our work, I'd like to say a few words about—"

Never one for pep talks, Buchar, after muttering an audible 'bullshit!' jumped to his feet and stalked from the room. Startled by the display, Noren, with a sneer forming on his face, watched as Buchar disappeared through the door.

From the start, Buchar kept to himself, eschewing conversation and remaining at this desk. On his third day, his focus produced results when digging into a remote corner of the Metrius software, Buchar saw something that quickened his pulse. The virus, he realized, contained a 'RAT,' computer-jargon for remote access tool, something, he mused, the terrorists had placed there to control the plants' operations. He was just about to probe deeper when he was interrupted by Irv Noren stepping into his cubicle to demand an update on his progress. Making minimal effort to conceal his irritation, Buchar placated Noren with just enough information to get him to leave him alone.

As Noren was departing, Buchar noticed something odd. Phillip D'Arnot, a Frenchman in the adjacent cubicle, seemed to be leaning over the wall that separated the two workspaces, apparently attempting to eavesdrop on his conversation with Noren. Later that evening a second troubling event occurred, when probing into the RAT program embedded in the Metrius software, a security alert flashed on Buchar's screen:

```
Intrusion alert! User "anonymous" is attempting to
access your filesystem.
```

Reacting quickly, Buchar logged into to the facility's network security program and saw that someone just seconds earlier had tried and failed to hack into his personal files. Thinking back to the eavesdropping incident of earlier that day, Buchar immediately suspected D'Arnot. The Frenchman had badgered Buchar with questions since the day he'd arrived. The most troubling moment took place a day earlier when Buchar, having left his desk for a few minutes, returned and found D'Arnot standing in his cubicle. Startled at seeing Buchar, he sputtered something about returning from the men's room and mistaking Buchar's cubicle for his. Not buying his explanation, Buchar said nothing, but resolved from that moment to take extraordinary precautions to secure his work. Henceforth he would encrypt his network files with a password that only he would know. And in direct defiance of established policy, he would preserve his most critical work not on the facility's secured network, but on a personal thumb drive that he kept with him at all times. To Buchar, the risk of an infiltrator sabotaging his work was too great to do otherwise. And if Irv Noren or anyone else didn't like it, they could go to hell.

On August 4th, Noren called a meeting and announced amid great fanfare that the security team from Britain had managed to isolate a chunk of executable code that they believed contained the virus. It was a critical breakthrough, Noren said. Buchar watching as others glad-handed the British team, sneered contemptuously. He'd done the same thing twenty-four hours earlier, but unsure of whom he could trust, had said nothing. More to the point, Buchar knew that isolating the executable code was only a modest step forward. The vile force behind the Metrius virus had made it clear that any attempt at disabling the virus within the reactors themselves would be detected, resulting in the immediate destruction of all three plants. The only way to disable the virus, Buchar knew, was through a *back door;* that is, to somehow find a way to hack into the Fourth Order's computer network and disable the virus at its source. A daunting, if not impossible task, to be sure.

The following day Buchar worked tirelessly. Throughout the afternoon and into the early hours, he pushed himself repeatedly to the edge of exhaustion, only to fall short each time. The breaking point came at 2 a.m. when, after another failed attempt, he pushed away from his desk and hurled his glasses to the floor. It couldn't be done. Not by him, or, he felt sure, by anyone else. At least not in time to stop the plants' destruction.

On the heels of a muttered 'fuck!' he made his way to the break room. After grabbing a beer that he'd smuggled into his lunch sack, he made his way back to his desk, then, as he'd done so often over the past 5 days, yanked Ray Trask's final note to Reid Temple from his shirt pocket and stared heavily at it.

ends just means tri ci

What was Trask, in the last moments of his life, trying to say? It maddened him to think that the note in his hand held the solution to the crisis, but he was unable to divine its meaning.

After eyeing the paper for a long, silent minute, he stuffed it back in his pocket. As he did, his mind shifted to the zealots responsible for this crisis. While he certainly felt contempt for the sect that had infected the Metrius software, he couldn't resist feeling a grudging admiration for their skill. Stumping the world's greatest computer scientists with their cryptography wasn't easy, and to this point anyway, they'd succeeded. His mind roamed over the group's odd name. What was the meaning of the Fourth Order? Could the name have a historical significance? If so, would understanding it get him any closer to unlocking the secret to the virus? With his analysis of the software going nowhere and just days until the plants were destroyed, there was nothing to lose in trying to find out.

On Monday, Buchar called Maddy Daniel. Would she be willing to meet him at the secure facility for lunch? At 1 p.m. the next day, Maddy, after running a gantlet of security checkpoints, made her way to facility's dining room. As she entered, Buchar, seated at a table in a far corner, waved her over.

Telling her he'd been busy with work, Buchar asked Maddy for an update on the latest news.

Chaos, she replied. The entire country was experiencing double-barreled panic. The Army and National Guard were under orders to evacuate everyone within five miles of the Poughkeepsie plant, but some were resisting, refusing to leave. To make things worse, she told him, rumors were rampant on the Internet, talk radio and cable news that the entire crisis was being manufactured by the governments of the U.S., France and Britain to crack down on civil liberties. The financial news was no better, she said. The terror had spread to Wall Street and the economy was tanking in much the same way it had following 9/11. Maddy shook her head. "It feels like the end times," she said. She then asked Buchar if he'd made any progress in cracking the Metrius virus.

"No," he said, exasperation marking his voice. "Without a breakthrough of some sort, I'm convinced the virus can't be cracked in time to save the plants." Noting Maddy's despair, he attempted to reassure her. "I'm not giving up," he said quickly. "I'm going to try something else."

Intrigued, Maddy asked what.

"I'm playing a hunch. There's someone I need to visit. Someone I met years ago with a deep background in early Middle Eastern history."

"Can't you reach him by phone?"

Buchar shook his head. "I've scoured public records trying to find a number for him. All I've got is a mailing address in Santa Barbara, a two hour drive from here. Which means I've got to find a way out of this joint."

"Can't you leave?"

"No, not with the security they've implemented. Anyone working on this project without a permanent security clearance is stuck here. And that's me."

"What are you going to do?"

"I've hatched a plan on how to get out of here tonight and hopefully return without anyone realizing I'm missing." Then, with his voice dropping to a hush, he leaned closer to Maddy. "There's something I want you to have." Reaching out with left hand, he tapped the side of his wrist watch. In a flash, the face flipped open, where inside, a small thumb drive was hidden.

After shooting a side-long glance around the room, he pressed it into Maddy's palm.

"What's this?" Maddy asked.

"A complete record of my attempts at cracking the virus ," he said, "and what I'm trying from this point forward. I don't trust anyone here, so I'm giving it to you, just in case."

Maddy eyed him with alarm. "Are you concerned for your safety?"

"You never know," he said, closing the cover to his watch. "But whatever happens, at least you'll have my information."

Maddy nodded solemnly. Thinking of the security obstacles she'd encountered just getting into the facility, Maddy asked him how he intended to get away. Buchar smiled, then without uttering a word, pointed at his eyes and blinked twice.

That night at 11p.m., Buchar, using techniques that he'd perfected over years of security work, tunnelled into the facility's computer security database. Then, navigating his way through filesystems, he found the directory where the digital signatures were stored. Defeating the encryption took some time, but he finally found the algorithm that generated the synthetic iris images for the plant's supervisors. Opening a folder labeled "i_noren," he quickly copied the image and sent it to a printer. Once the image was printed and then copied to a plastic sheet, Buchar, using a pen knife, lifted the printed image, then carefully placed the images over a pair of contacts he sometimes wore. After placing the lenses in his eyes, he made his way to an exit door, then with his heart pounding, positioned himself in front of the iris scanner. The optical scanner, sensing that the individual before it was Irv Noren, signaled for the door to open. 'Son of a bitch,' Buchar muttered to himself as he removed the contacts. It worked!

Racing up Interstate 10 to Santa Barbara, Buchar's mind shifted to the man he was journeying to meet. He'd first encountered Aban Ashif years earlier at a seminar and had struck up a casual friendship with him. Despite not being affiliated with a university, Ashif was reputed to be one of the world's foremost authorities on esoteric Middle Eastern history. Buchar had found him a bit eccentric – he wore his stringy hair down to his shoulders, talked incessantly of his gun collection and had a nervous habit of constantly squinching one eye open and shut. But there was no denying his charisma or his intelligence and the two had remained in touch for a few years until losing contact. Could Ashif, with his extensive knowledge, provide a clue to the terrorist sect and its odd name?

Just over two hours later, Buchar arrived in Santa Barbara. Following directions he'd downloaded from the Internet, he made his way through the winding roads and oak-studded hills of central California before finally pulling up in front of a large Tudor house fronted by a massive iron gate. Pushing the gate's intercom button, he waited for a response. Getting none, he tried again. A long minute later, a voice called out.

"Who in hell is it?"

"It's Liam. Liam Buchar."

"I don't know a Liam Buchar. It's the middle of the night. Go away."

"We met a few years ago."

"I said go away."

"It was at a seminar on Middle Eastern history."

The line fell silent.

"It's Liam Buchar from the university."

"What do you want?"

"To speak with you. I'm working on the Metrius crisis."

"I don't know what you're talking about."

"The Metrius crisis. You must have heard about it. It's all over the news."

"I have not."

"It's critical that I speak with you."

"About what?"

"The Middle East."

After a long pause, followed by a deep sigh, a buzzer sounded. A moment later, the heavy brass gate clanked noisily, then slowly began to creak open.

Gunning his engine, Buchar wound his way up the twisting road toward the house. Initially impressed at the house's size, upon drawing near, Buchar was stunned at the level of disrepair. Paint was peeling, shutters hung askew and shingles on the roof were broken revealing wooden supports beneath. The grounds were no better, with an overgrowth of scrub and a pond in the front filled with brackish water and floating trash.

Once he'd parked, Buchar made his way to the front door and knocked. He was greeted by a man of about thirty with a body like stacked lumber who introduced himself as Dorian, who then pointed him to the study where Ashif would greet him.

As he waited, Buchar took in his surroundings. In the center of the room stood a table with a chessboard, with pieces arranged to suggest a game was currently in progress. Heavy wooden bookcases stuffed with weighty tomes lined the wall, but the books within were covered with dust and a number of the shelves had collapsed under the weight of the volumes. In a far corner stood a locked cabinet containing all manner of large and small firearms, while overhead, a ceiling fan creaked noisily. In the corner was a small elevator, obviously used to transport someone with an infirmity from an upper floor.

After waiting for almost twenty minutes, Buchar heard the clatter of metal. Turning to his right, he watched as the elevator lowered to the ground floor. A moment later, a shriveled man in a wheelchair with a wrinkled Shar-pei face, a bald dome and stringy wisps of side hair that fell to his shoulders, was rolled into the room by Dorian. Buchar could scarcely believe that the wasted and drawn figure before him was the robust man he'd met less than ten years earlier. After pushing the old man to the center of the room where he could greet Buchar, Dorian retreated to a far corner where he stood with his arms crossed, eyeing Liam steadily.

Unsure of the greeting he'd receive, Buchar hesitantly extended his hand. To his surprise, the old man greeted him warmly, the deep furrows of his face disappearing into a wide smile that revealed a mouth full of yellow teeth.

"Liam," Ashif said, extending his hand. 'I remember you now. Forgive me for sounding so unwelcoming. I was asleep when you rang. I get very few visitors these days. And my deteriorating body has made me pretty grouchy."

Relieved, Buchar shook his hand, then sat down across from the old man's wheelchair.

"I'm sorry to trouble you at this hour, but it's important." Buchar's eyes settled on the cabinet at the far end the room. "I see you haven't lost your interest in firearms," he said.

"One of the few passions that hasn't deserted me," Ashif replied.

"I hope there's another one that hasn't," Buchar said. There was a threat against nuclear plants in the U.S., Britain and France, Buchar told him. Three great cities were about to be destroyed and possibly millions killed if he didn't complete his work. His efforts at cracking the worm had failed and he was now reduced to grasping at straws.

The terrorists called themselves the Fourth Order. Ashif knew more than any man alive about esoteric Middle Eastern history. Did the group's name mean anything to him?

As he sat, Ashif twirled a lock of stringy, unwashed hair between his thumb and forefinger, as if trying to remember. A moment later, his eyes brightened.

"The First Order," he said finally.

"What?"

The old man waved his hand dismissively. "On second thought, forget it. There's probably no connection. I'd just be wasting your time."

"I've come all this way," Buchar replied. "Let me hear what you have to say."

Ashif shrugged, "Okay. During the first Crusade, there was a Muslim sect known as the Seljuks that was founded by a Turkish nomad named Hassan Hatash." The old man fell mute for a moment. "Ok," he said finally, "I've got it now. Sometime around 1097, Hatash and his sect, outraged by atrocities committed by Christians against Muslims, vowed to resist the invaders."

"Nothing unique about that."

"No, but their methods were. To the Seljuks, the Quran was infallible. As a result, they vowed to resist the invaders in a way that was consistent with their interpretation of Muslim law. Using the Prophet Muhammad's injunction to mercy and forgiveness as their foundation, the Seljuks vowed to fight the invaders only when attacked and resisted calls to engage in any actions they felt violated

Sharia law."

"How does this relate—"

"Let me finish," Ashif said, silencing Buchar with a wave of his hand. "To resist the invaders and to do it in a moral way, the Seljuks established a pair of decrees that came to be known as 'orders.'"

Buchar heart quickened. "They called their decrees 'orders'?"

"They did," Ashif replied. "The first order, in direct response to the cruelty they'd seen committed by the crusaders, mandated that the Christians, though considered infidels, were to be viewed first as humans and therefore, not subject to immoral treatment. That decree was soon followed by a second order that said once the invaders were defeated, the truly repentant among them would be allowed to co-exist with Muslims in the Holy Land so long as no attempt was made to convert them to Christianity."

"Pretty progressive stuff, especially considering the brutality of the time."

"It was," Ashif replied. "And it generated substantial controversy among Muslims, many of whom viewed the Europeans as sub-human and worthy of nothing but death. And to many others, Hatash was derided as naïve and simplistic. But due to its uniqueness, Hatash's philosophy attracted considerable attention and soon gained a substantial following. And over time, some saw him as a great teacher. However, as the brutality of the Christians escalated during the First Crusade, Hatash renounced some of his earlier views and adopted a harder line toward the invaders. Anyway, sometime around 1099, Hatash and the Seljuks were captured by the Christians and taken prisoner. The Christians then proceeded to torture Hatash before brutally killing him."

"And the Seljuks?"

"Them too."

"So much for reconciliation," Buchar said.

"The sect was killed off and as far as I or anyone knows, that's the end of the story." The old man shrugged. "We're talking about something that happened almost a thousand years ago. There can't be a connection to nuclear power plants in the twenty-first century."

Buchar eyed him curiously. "There was never a successive order or orders?"

"No." The old man waved his hand again. "I'm sorry I couldn't be of more help. I'm afraid you've come all this way for nothing." Then with his eyes brightening, Ashif gestured toward the weapons cabinet in the corner. "Want to look at my guns?" he asked.

Buchar declined.

"Then how about a game of chess?"

Buchar got to his feet. "There's no time." Liam then thanked the old man and left. As he drove away, Buchar's mind was fixed on something Ashif had said, specifically about the first order issued by the Seljuks in 1099. Could there a link, however distant, between that progressive group and the radical sect that today threatened the lives of millions? A link that however tenuous, could not be totally obscured by a thousand years of history? A connection that even Ashif himself wasn't aware of? He glanced at his watch. 2:07 a.m. Reaching for his phone, he punched in a number. A moment later, a man, sounding groggy and disoriented, answered.

"Art," Buchar said, his voice rising, "I need access to the UC Santa Barbara Library of Antiquities. And I need it now!"

Chapter 31

At 2:20 a.m., Liam Buchar raced into the parking lot of the University of Santa Barbara where he was met by a security guard. "I got a call from the head of university security," the guard said, his flashlight trained on Buchar's face. "You the guy who wants access to the library?" Buchar nodded. Signaling for Buchar to follow him, the two men walked to the south end of the campus.

Once inside the library, Buchar thanked the guard and immediately made his way to the directory, which indicated that the university's collection of ancient texts was kept on the third floor. Reaching the top of the stairs, Buchar saw that the room was stuffed from floor to ceiling with bulging bookcases reeking of mildew and age. Because most of the overhead lights had burned out and not been replaced, the room was cloaked in a funereal gloom.

Squinting to penetrate the room's darkness, Buchar spotted a book shelf labeled "Early Middle Eastern History." For the next hour, he gingerly picked his way through books in various stages of disintegration, while outside, a soft rain began to fall.

After an hour of leafing through dozens of tomes, he saw something that looked promising: a large, cloth-bound volume with a crumbling spine that read *Ancient Near East*. Stepping closer to the room's solitary light source, Buchar flipped gingerly through the book's crumbling pages, searching for something, *anything,* that might provide a clue to the mystery of the Fourth Order. He was just about to give up when something stopped him cold. In a chapter on the early Crusades, the book contained a reference to the Seljuks and the First Order mentioned by Ashif. Absorbed now, Buchar read on and moments later, was stunned by what he found. Ashif was *wrong* …a sect *had* sprung up in Palestine in the early years of the 20th century using the original Seljuks as their inspiration!

So immersed was Buchar by what he read, that at first he didn't notice the creaking of the stairwell that lead to the room. When his concentration broke and he finally looked up, he saw a shadowy figure slide past the doorway, then disappear behind a bookcase at the far end of the room. Or did he? Days of stress and fatigue had taken their toll, leaving him unsure of his senses. With his heart pounding, Buchar called out. "Is someone there?"

Silence.

"Is it the security guard?"

Silence.

Unnerved, Buchar delicately closed the book, tucked it under his arm. then with light steps, eased to the far side of the room and peered through the gloom hoping to see if someone was there.

He saw nothing.

Anxiously, he tip-toed to the stairs, made his way down and hurried to the front of the building, where he spotted the security guard napping on a bench beneath a street lamp. Hearing Buchar approach, he awakened with a start.

"Find what you were looking for?" he asked groggily.

"I think so," Buchar replied. He then asked if there was someone else in the building other than himself.

"Not a soul," he replied, standing up. "No one in his right mind," he said eyeing Buchar steadily, "would be out at this hour." Then spying the volume in Buchar's hand, he shook his head. "Sorry sir, but that's university property. You can't take it with you."

Buchar shot a glance at his watch. It was 3:40 a.m. Realizing he had just over two hours to get back to the secure facility before he was detected, Buchar appealed to the guard. "Look," he said, a pleading in his voice. "I'm a professor at the University of Santa Cruz. I'm working on the Metrius crisis. I have to return to Los Angeles right now or—"

"Nope," the watchman said, reaching to take the book from Buchar's hand, "this can't—"

A powerful blow from Buchar's right hand sent the guard crashing to the cement. Then, after mouthing 'sorry' at the unconscious figure on the pavement, Buchar dashed for his car.

Chapter 32

Wednesday August 9th. 3:50 am PDT

For the next two hours, Buchar raced the length of California Highway 1 at speeds of over ninety miles an hour. In one respect, he felt lucky. With sunrise still more that two hours away, cops, whom he hated with the same vehemence he felt for the government, were scarce. He also knew that with every passing minute, his chances of returning to the secure government facility undetected were diminished. Irv Noren, a notorious early riser, usually arrived at the facility by 6 a.m. sharp. If Buchar didn't beat him to the entrance, the security system, thinking that Noren had left earlier that evening and then returned the next morning, would admit Noren, thereby preventing Buchar from gaining entry and leaving him stranded outside. His only hope was to beat Noren to the plant, get inside, then fake another departure in order to clear the system for Noren's actual entry.

Racing into the plant at 5:57, Buchar scanned the parking lot, then felt his spirits plunge. There, in its usual spot, was Noren's vehicle. Suppressing a shudder, Buchar parked his car, then knowing what awaited him, made his way toward the entry door with a leaden stride.

He was just approaching the entrance, when he saw something that quickened his hopes. Instead of entering the plant, Noren, just steps from the entry door, had stopped to speak with a colleague. Thinking it might be still possible to escape detection, Buchar dashed for a side entrance and raced up to the iris scanner. Seconds later, Noren, bidding his colleague goodbye, did the same. With halting breaths, Buchar confronted the scanner and opened his eyes wide, desperate to be admitted.

Nothing.

Assuming that Noren had beat him to the scanner, thus blocking his entry, Buchar gulped heavily. Then it hit him. He'd forgotten to place the contact lenses with Noren's iris images in his eyes! Frantically, Buchar pulled the contacts from his pocket, hurriedly placed them over his eyes, then faced the scanner. To his relief, the door unlocked. Dashing in, Buchar then made an about face and confronted the scanner again as if to exit, praying that Noren had not yet reached the entry door himself. The scanner, believing that Buchar was actually Noren attempting to exit, unlocked once again as Buchar, ducking below the scanner itself and feigning an exit, remained inside the facility. A split-second later, Noren, facing the scanner at the main entry door, was admitted. With just seconds to spare, Buchar had made it inside, undetected.

Itching to resume his investigation of the newly acquired book, Buchar, feigning illness, returned to his room at 9 a.m. and began pouring over its contents. Forty minutes later, he eased back in his chair, his mind spinning. What had he learned? That Ashif was mistaken. The radical order established by Hatash had *not* died out following the crushing of his sect by the Christians in 1097. As the book made clear, when it came to the Middle East, there were no codas, only constants. Because in 1905, almost a thousand years following the assassination of Hatash, a group, also calling themselves the Seljuks, sprung up in Palestine. Unlike the original sect overseen by the benevolent Hatash, this incarnation, though claiming Hatash as its inspiration, was led by a brutal zealot named Kiril Fortos. Fortos, who claimed to be the true inheritor of Hatash's legacy, dispensed with the original Seljuk mission of rehabilitating Christians and instead launched a fiery crusade of exterminating anyone who didn't adhere to Sharia law from the Holy Land. Once established, the reconstructed Seljuks, mimicking the approach of their namesake if not their humanity, issued a set of principles which they called the Third Order!

As he read on, Buchar learned that the Third Order, which was issued in 1907, consisted of two halves. The first, authored in Persian, outlined in blunt and coarse terms the sect's goal of expelling infidels from the Middle East. Any who resisted would be killed. Fascinating stuff to be sure, Buchar thought, but nothing compared to what followed. The communique's second half, which outlined the bloody tactics the group would utilize to 'cleanse' the Holy Land of infidels was issued in coded form, using the *Trithemius Cipher*, an ancient form of cryptology that was lost to time.

Reaching for his laptop, Buchar quickly entered "Trithemius Cipher" into a browser. This is what he saw:

The Trithemius Cipher – *One of the great mysteries of the middle ages, the Trithemius Cipher was an ancient method of encoding messages using the tabula recta, a form of cryptography that removes letter frequencies to encode information. It was created by the 15th century occultist and reputed conjurer of the dead Johanne Trithemius (1462 – 1516), (pronounced Try-tay-me-us). Trithemius is perhaps best known as the author of "Steganographia" a book that circulated throughout Europe in manuscript form for a century before finally being published in Frankfurt. For over a hundred years, it was widely believed that Steganographia contained a formula for conjuring the dead. But because its contents were in coded form, no one could be sure, despite effort by scholars to unlock its secrets. The work was widely attacked by religious leaders and was soon added to the Index Librorum Prohibitorum, the Catholic Church's list of condemned books and was not removed from the list until the early 1900's."*

Armed with this new information, Buchar's mind began to race. Baffling officials a century earlier with a mysterious form of cryptography was one thing. But could an ancient method of obscuring words and information from prying eyes be applied to modern computer technology? It was a known fact that from the day the first mainframe was rolled out, computer science had relied on cryptographic algorithms to protect data and secure communications, Had a 21st century mind, in a cyber-nod to Fortos, applied cryptographic principles invented over 400 years ago to modern computer code, convinced that a medieval shaman and his mysterious cipher were lost to time?

Turning back to his book, Buchar skipped ahead to a section

addressing the latter-day Seljuks and their use of the cipher to obscure the meaning of their communique, which they called the Third Order.

"After issuing the Third Order, the Seljuks began a series of attacks on non-Muslims in 1906, brutally slaughtering hundreds. In an effort to stop the killing, police worked furiously to crack the communiques' coded half. Finally, after months of effort, someone realized that the cryptography was created hundreds of years earlier by Johanne Trithemius and were finally able to decode it. Doing so revealed the sect's murderous designs on non-Muslims in the Holy Land, ultimately leading to their capture. Kiril Fortos, counting on the obscurity of the Trithemius Cipher to shield him, (and in an act of supreme hubris), added his name to the final line of the coded half of the communique. Once the code was cracked, he, along with other members of the sect, was identified, tracked down, tried and convicted of his crimes. According to those present, moments before he was hanged in Anotolia on September 12, 1907, Fortos last words were "The ends justified my means!"

With a quick motion, Buchar yanked Ray Trask's note from his pocket and re-read it. It suddenly made sense. Trask, in the final moments of his life, was attempting to alert Reid Temple to a connection between the Trithemius Cipher, Forto's methodology and the Metrius virus! With his senses at full alert, Buchar jumped to his feet and began to stalk the length of the room. As improbable as it once seemed, it was now likely that a 15th century occultist and practitioner of black magic could provide the key to unlocking the mystery of the Fourth Order and it's destructive plan for the world! If so, he had just five days to find out.

When Buchar returned to his desk, he found a note from Noren, saying he wanted to see him. In no mood for Noren or any of his games, Buchar nonetheless made his way down the long hallway towards his office. As he approached Noren's office, Buchar passed Phillip D'Arnot, who was wearing a sly expression, just exiting.

Once inside, Noren, following a gruff hello, motioned Buchar to a chair. Someone a few hours earlier, he said, had hacked into the facility's security programs. Did Buchar know anything about it?

"Nope," Buchar replied. "Why do you ask?"

"Where were you last night?"

Buchar snorted dismissively. "Asleep."

"Are you sure?"

"Let's cut the shit," Buchar said with his anger cresting. "What are you driving at?"

"Someone knocked on your door last night, but there was no response."

"I'm a heavy sleeper," Buchar shot back. "What the fuck's this about?"

"For the time being," Noren replied, "nothing. But we're examining tapes from all the security cameras. If someone left the facility without authorization, federal charges will be leveled against the person responsible. Which means, if convicted, jail time and a possible charge of sedition." Noren fixed Buchar with an accusatory stare. "Now, is there anything you have to say?" Buchar shook his head.

"Ok," Noren said, "that will be all, for now."

Fucking right, that's all, Buchar thought as he stalked from

Noren's office. He'd had enough. Tonight he would once again escape the facility. And this time, he wouldn't be back.

Chapter 33

By Wednesday, Maddy's spirits were in free-fall. In just minutes, she would take her place at the anchor desk and report of a stunning development in the Metrius crisis. According to a leak from a high-level source at the State Department, all efforts at cracking the Metrius virus had failed. And while attempts were ongoing, no one was optimistic that the virus could be cracked in time to prevent the plants from detonating. To Maddy, it seemed unbelievable. In just five days, the world would experience a catastrophe that sounded more like a plotline from a cheesy disaster movie than a real-life event.

At the end of her newscast, Pete Martin pushed a manila envelope across the desk to Maddy. When she opened it, she saw it was the autopsy report on Mirit Taham along with a snapshot of his face. After skimming it in her office, Maddy reached for her phone. When Amber came on the line, she explained she had the autopsy report.

"It was Polonium," she said, "a highly toxic element. It causes death virtually 100% of the time. Once it's ingested, there's virtually no way to decontaminate someone that's been poisoned."

Amber asked how it ended up in her brother's body.

"Someone probably spiked his drink or added it to his food," Maddy said. "It's virtually tasteless and odorless."

Maddy eyed the gruesome photo that accompanied the autopsy

report, then asked Amber if she'd be willing to view it to conclusively identify her brother. Amber said yes. As she hung up the phone, Maddy heard the sound of sobbing.

Chapter 34

On Wednesday night, using the same set of altered contact lenses he'd used earlier, Buchar fled the secure facility for the final time. Five hours later armed with his book on Middle Eastern history and a thumb drive containing his files, he arrived in Santa Cruz. Returning home was a risk and he knew it. U.S security agencies, noticing his absence, would be on his trail by morning. His only hope was to apply what he'd learned about the latter-day Seljuks and the Trithemius Cipher to the Metrius virus and end the threat before they found him.

Once at home, his first act was to phone Maddy, telling her of his whereabouts and his growing hope at solving the crisis. Just before hanging up, Maddy mentioned that she had been contacted by Littleton Barry. He was being vilified in the press over the crisis, and was desperate to share his side of the story. As a result, Maddy told Buchar, she had an appointment with Barry the following day to conduct an interview that would air the on her newscast.

After ringing off, Buchar brewed a pot of strong black coffee then made his way to his desk. He had much to do. First on his list was learning everything he could about Johanne Trithemius and his cipher. Opening a browser, he entered the name of the ancient cryptographer into a search engine and eased back in his chair. What he saw surprised him. In addition to a smattering of sites that provided historical information on Trithemius, there were dozens specializing on occultism that covered Trithemius and his supposed connection to the supernatural. Skipping over these, he scoured the web for another few minutes before landing on a web page that approached the cipher from a mathematical perspective.

"Goddam clever son of a bitch," Buchar muttered as he learned more about Trithemius and his work. Ciphers that utilized alphabetic substitution or symbols for words were nothing new. But Trithemius had confounded everyone by substituting values for letters and most impressively, doing it without a key. Without a key, which made coded text indecipherable, scholars had no choice but to try to defeat the cryptography, a virtually impossible task for men of the middle-ages. No wonder, Buchar mused, it had taken so long to divine the meaning of Trithemius' coded writings.

After an hour had passed, Buchar, feeling jittery from all the coffee he'd consumed, returned to the kitchen for a beer. After flipping the bottle cap in the general direction of the trash container, he leaned against the sink, deep in thought. It was now evident that the Fourth Order was using the Trithemius Cipher to encrypt the Metrius virus. Still, cracking it wouldn't be easy. Numeric patterns had evolved over the centuries and something obvious to a person in the 15th century would be as alien as Sanskrit to someone today. And cracking it was only the first step. The radiation leak over Poughkeepsie made it clear that the Fourth Order's claim of having complete control over the reactors and their processes was no empty boast. Which meant that any direct attempt to disable the virus would be detected, resulting in the immediate destruction of all three plants. The only way to safely break the Fourth Order's hold on the reactors, Buchar knew, was to mount a reverse attack on the group's computer systems with a program of his own that would destroy their work and preserve the plants. It wouldn't be easy, but still, Buchar had hope. After weeks of grinding frustration, he, at last, had something to go on.

For the next three hours, he sat fixed at his desk, working at a frantic pace. Shortly before 1 a.m., he saw something in an encrypted area of the Metrius code that seemed out of place. Encouraged, he probed deeper, digging into the darkest corners of the software for anything that might be linked to the virus. A half-hour later, he spotted something that quickened his pulse. Buried in the code was a numeric pattern that to the naked eye, made no sense. Was this the link he'd been seeking?

Convinced he was closing in on the virus, he pressed on. So complete was his absorption that hours passed before, feeling exhausted, he eased back in his chair and stretched deeply. The room, with the exception of a bluish glow coming from his computer screen, was swallowed by darkness On a far wall where the shadows grew thicker, he could just make out a clock. It said 3:45 a.m.

What was that?

Reacting to a sharp sound coming from outside, he flinched, the sudden motion sending his glasses clattering loudly to his desktop.

With stealthful steps, he moved to window. Easing the curtain back, he saw that rain was pelting the courtyard, while in the distance, storm clouds raked the Santa Cruz mountains as flashes of lightning stabbed the sky.

Probably a tree branch scraping against the roof.

With a heavy sigh, he eased his glasses back on and turned back to his computer. He drilled deeper and deeper into the source code and soon made a startling discovery: the Metrius virus was generating an alphabetic substitution, the same technique used by Trithemius! No wonder the best computer minds in the world hadn't been able to unlock the secret to the virus…the ancient mystic's clever methodology made the malware that infected the Metrius source code look like a random data string. In a flash moment, it hit him: the Metrius computer virus could now be cracked!

For the next hour, he worked his way through the virus' encrypted layers, dropping electronic breadcrumbs in the form of notes that he could use to disable the virus.

Shortly after 4 a.m. Buchar stumbled upon something that left him breathless and trembling. He was removing letter frequencies from a section of ciphertext, when a random code string appeared. After applying the Trithemius Cipher to the string, he lurched back in his chair, stunned at what he saw. There, encoded in a remote corner of the Metrius source code, the evil mind behind the plot to blackmail the world had, in a moment of breathtaking hubris that contained ghostly echoes of an earlier time, *had spelled out his name!*

Shocked by what he saw, Buchar grabbed his phone. He had to

stop her before it was too late! It wasn't until he felt the needle plunge into the soft flesh of his neck that he realized he wasn't alone in the room.

Chapter 35

August 10th

At 10 a.m. Thursday, a GBS remote truck carrying Maddy and members of her crew pulled up in front of Barry Towers, an imposing edifice of glass and steel that loomed over downtown Los Angeles. After unloading their equipment, they hopped an elevator to the twenty-first floor, where, after navigating their way down a long hallway and through a set of double doors, Maddy announced herself to Littleton Barry's executive secretary.

The woman, looking chagrined, apologized to Maddy. "I'm sorry Ms. Daniel, but you just missed him," she said. "Sahn Rameer burst through the door just minutes ago asking to see Mr. Barry. I heard the two of them talking in hushed tones, then a moment later, they rushed from the room. Mr. Barry asked me to apologize to you."

Uncertain of whether to wait in the hope Barry might return or simply leave, Maddy weighed her options. Finally, signaling to her colleagues that it was time to go, Maddy and her crew made their way downstairs. As they began loading up their equipment, Maddy, needing to call the GBS news department to inform them of the cancellation, pulled out her cell phone. At that moment, a large black car lurched from the building's underground garage with tires squealing, then after swerving and narrowly missing the GBS truck, careened crazily down Spring Street at a high speed. Startled by the commotion, Maddy looked up from her phone and was stunned by what she saw. Seated in the back seat of the racing vehicle was Sahn Rameer. Riding shotgun was Littleton Barry. And behind the wheel, was a jug-eared man in a Panama hat.

Chapter 36

Stunned at seeing Littleton Barry and Sahn Rameer with the man who'd given the explosive satchel to Alison, Maddy jumped in the remote truck and ordered a member of the crew to follow the speeding car. For the next three minutes, they gave chase, nearly overtaking the vehicle before finally being halted by a funeral procession at Jefferson Street. Back at the GBS studios, Maddy struggled to make sense of what she'd just seen. What were Littleton Barry and Sahn Rameer doing with a murderer? Did they know of his involvement in Alison's death? Sahn Rameer's direct involvement in the charity was no secret. Could she now assume that Littleton Barry knew of the shady business taking place there as well? While it seemed incredible, could Barry, -- and given his radical past, Sahn Rameer -- be working together to sabotage Metrius? If so, why?

Something else was plaguing Maddy. For hours, desperate for an update on his progress, she'd tried repeatedly to reach Liam Buchar. But each time she was greeted by his voicemail and although she'd left message after message pleading with him to contact her, he'd never called back.

With doubts and fears swarming around her like gnats she couldn't kill, Maddy sat, unsure of what to do. She desperately needed to talk to someone, but with Reid dead, Barry and Rameer consorting with a killer and Buchar missing, it seemed she had nowhere to turn. Then it hit her: there was one person that Reid believed in completely, the man who'd saved his life and remained by her side in the dark hours following his death. Grabbing her phone, she hurriedly punched in Jason DeMir's number.

At 7:30 that night, Maddy pulled up in front of a brick townhouse in Century City, west of Los Angeles. After answering the door, Jason gave her a warm hug and showed her into the living area. After declining his offer of coffee, she sat down opposite him and recounted the circumstances of her visit to Littleton Barry just hours earlier and the murderer he was seen with. Listening intently to her words, Jason sat with an expression of incredulity, as if trying to wrap his mind around what he'd just heard. When she was done, he spoke, his words tumbling forth in a halting cadence " "I...I...I can't believe this," he said. "Littleton, involved in murder and the sabotage of Metrius?" He shook his head. "Have you informed the police of what you saw today?

"You bet."

Jason shook his head. "I don't get it Maddy," he said. "I was with Littleton when he first learned of the sabotage of the Metrius deployments. He appeared devastated."

"What about Sahn Rameer?" Maddy asked. "With his background, didn't anyone question his involvement in Metrius?"

"We knew he was once associated with questionable people," DeMir replied, "but Littleton checked and was convinced he could be trusted. He had complete faith in him."

DeMir asked about the secret facility near where Reid was killed. How had Maddy learned of it?

"Rita Sessions told Alison," Maddy replied. "She handled procurement for the Metrius Foundation. She learned of materials being ordered and delivered there. And of personnel disappearing from their normal jobs and then turning up there to work."

"Do the police know about it?"

Maddy nodded. "They checked on it," she said. "As it turns out, the facility was torched shortly after Reid's death hit the news. There's nothing but rubble there now. They're trying to trace it, but ownership was obscured through shell companies that were set up to hide it."

Jason ran a hand nervously through his hair. "I was listening to news reports on the crisis before you arrived," he said. "Things are getting worse. And now this."

"For awhile there," Maddy said, "I had hope." She then told DeMir of her association with Liam Buchar and his efforts at solving the crisis.

"What happened?"

"Just like that," Maddy said, snapping her fingers, "he's disappeared. With just four days left, he's vanished." She shook her head. "He was my best hope."

"Well," Jason said rising to his feet. "we may not be able to stop the plants from igniting, but we sure as hell can hold the people behind this madness for their actions. The minute you leave, I'll get the board of directors on the phone and tell them what I've learned.

They'll undoubtedly be interested in learning that Barry Inc. is being used as a criminal enterprise for terrorists."

Feeling relieved to have shared her story with Jason, Maddy rose, gave him a deep hug, then started for the door "It's funny," Maddy said, stopping and turning to Jason, "but I feel relieved. If I didn't talk to someone, I thought I would bust." She laughed a sardonic laugh. "Feeling relief with the world about to explode. Sounds crazy, doesn't it?"

"We're all human Maddy," Jason replied, a softness showing in his eyes. "It's important to know there's someone we can trust."

Nodding, Maddy said goodnight and made her way outside. With her mind still on the day's events, she never noticed the large black SUV parked a few yards away, nor the hulking, hooded figure behind the wheel who, once she'd driven away, quickly made his way to the rear of DeMir's home and lifted the window.

Chapter 37

Saturday August 12th

On Saturday, with just two days left before the Metrius plants were scheduled to detonate, the crisis atmosphere that gripped the United States and Europe reached hideous new heights. Nuclear physicists and meteorologists in the U.S. and Europe issued a joint statement estimating that, depending on weather conditions prevalent at the time the plants exploded, nuclear fallout from the three contaminated plants could extend up to fifty miles, Immediately, evacuation zones surrounding the plants in all three countries were extended and images of residents clogging highways and others battling police to remain in their homes, glutted the airwaves. Even areas hundreds of miles removed from the Metrius reactors weren't spared the chaos as terrified people descended upon drug stores for potassium pills and hardware and grocery stores for generators, water purification kits, face masks and canned goods.

Saturday, after trying and failing again to reach Liam Buchar, Maddy pulled the thumb drive he'd given her from her purse and plugged it into her laptop. Scanning its contents, she realized that Buchar, beginning with his first day at the secure facility, had maintained a meticulous record of his efforts at solving the Metrius crisis. Most entries were highly technical and far beyond Maddy's understanding. But the final entry, made just minutes before Buchar met Maddy for lunch that final day, proved to be most interesting: *August 8th – Depart skiff tonight. See Aban Ashif, 8745 Mission Canyon Road, Santa Barbara.*

Maddy's mind flashed back to her lunch conversation with Buchar and how downcast he'd been. The threat against the reactors couldn't be prevented, he'd said. At least 'not in time to stop the plants from exploding.' But when she spoke to him the final time, something had changed. 'I'm onto something,' he told her. 'Just give me a little time.' Maddy's eyes again fell on the final entry in his diary. Had Aban Ashif, whoever he was, shared something with Buchar that shed light on the crisis? Something that accounted for Buchar's optimism at halting the destruction of the plants? Maddy reached for her keyboard and scoured phone directories for Santa Barbara. After failing to find a phone number for Ashif, she knew there was only one thing to do: it might be a wild goose chase, but she would visit Aban Ashif the following day.

At 12:30, carrying the autopsy report and photograph given to her by Pete Martin, Maddy pulled up in front of Amber's house. As Amber greeted her at the door. a special report blared from a television in the living room.

"Dear God," Amber said switching off the TV. "Every update seems worse that the one before."

Maddy nodded. "Everybody's freaking out," she said. "Even the three impacted government's appear to be panicking. We're getting reports in the newsroom that the Brits and the French are about to announce they're ready to comply with the terrorists demands."

"How can they?" Amber asked, incredulously. "That would take months. And what makes anyone think the Israeli's would go along with it?"

Maddy nodded. "I know. But that's how insane things are right now." Then guiding Amber to the sofa, Maddy handed her the photo of the man at the morgue. Was that her brother?

Taking the picture hesitantly, Amber eyed it, then with her face registering horror, flung it to the floor. A moment later, she began to sob.

"Yes, that's Marit," she said, her face buried in her hands. "Is that what they did to him?"

Maddy nodded grimly. She reached for the autopsy report and handed it to Amber who examined it, an expression of despair marking her face. When she was done, she fell back to the couch. "Reassure me Maddy," she said. "Please tell me that my brother didn't die for nothing?"

"A day or two ago, I might've been able to comfort you," Maddy replied. "But now, I'm just not sure." Noting Amber's questioning look, Maddy told her of her relationship with Liam Buchar and his work on Metrius. She explained that Buchar had disappeared just when he appeared to be on the verge of solving the crisis.

"Disappeared!" Amber replied. "Are you afraid he's been harmed?"

Maddy nodded, then mentioned that she planned to visit the last person to see Buchar before he disappeared the following day.

"Who?"

Maddy pulled a piece of paper from her blouse pocket and unfolded it. "Someone named Aban Ashif," Maddy replied, reading the name on the paper. She then passed the note to Amber, who eyed it for a long, silent moment. Amber then passed the paper back to Maddy, who bid her goodbye.

Once back home, Maddy, wanting to inform Jason DeMir of her trip to see Aban Ashif, dialed his work number, But instead of reaching DeMir, Maddy was connected to a co-worker who told her that Jason was in the hospital after being seriously assaulted during a home invasion the night before. Ringing the hospital, Maddy was connected to DeMir, who sounding faint, came on the line.

"My god Jason," she said, "what happened?"

DeMir opened his mouth to speak but his voice was choked off by emotion. After clearing his throat, he started again. "Shortly after you left, a man…." he said, his voice halting, 'broke in through a bedroom window and attacked me."

"Are you okay?"

"Well, I'm lucky to be alive. Fortunately, I heard the window being raised. I confronted him and we fought. Sometime during the fight I was stabbed in my shoulder. After struggling for I don't know how long, I shouted for help. I guess that scared him away."

"Are you badly hurt?"

"I've lost a lot of blood, but I guess I'm okay."

Stunned by this latest development, Maddy fell silent. After being reassured by Jason that he would be fine, she rang off, making no mention of her planned visit to Aban Ashif.

On Sunday August 13th, the united front displayed to the world by the United States. Britain and France began a very public disintegration. With just one day left before the expiration of the Fourth Order's deadline, the besieged countries, realizing that a technological solution to the crisis wouldn't be forthcoming and sensing the futility of bargaining as a group, retreated into an every-country-to-itself posture. In a last minute gambit designed to spare them their fate, England's House of Commons adopted an emergency resolution agreeing to every condition laid down by the Fourth Order. In Paris, the Assemblee Nationale, in a unanimous vote, issued a declaration of full support for the Palestinian Authority and demanded that the United Nations immediately undertake steps to create a single Palestinian state to stretch from the Jordan River to the Mediterranean. In the United States, Republican Congressional leaders, adopting a more confrontational approach, urged the president to publicly state that the United States would launch a nuclear strike against Palestinian lands in the Middle East if the reactor in Poughkeepsie, New York was destroyed. The president, after labeling the plan as insane, did agree to place the nation's nuclear arsenal at full alert in the event that one of the nation's adversaries, mindful of the chaos that would follow a nuclear cataclysm, decided to launch a pre-emptive attack on the United States. All the while, the world waited anxiously for a response from the Fourth Order to the desperate proposals. None was forthcoming.

And so it was that with a deepening sense of despair, Maddy pulled up in front of a large, decaying house in Santa Barbara on the morning of August 13th to see if Aban Ashif could shed any light on the disappearance of Liam Buchar. After convincing the person on the other end of the gate's intercom that she was an acquaintance of Buchar's, she was greeted at the front door by the same man that Buchar had encountered just six days earlier, the hulking Dorian. Once inside, he directed Maddy to the study where Ashif would greet her.

As she waited, Maddy made her way around the study, intently studying the books that lined the room's deteriorating shelves. Then, with the ticking of a grandfather's clock as the only sound in the room, she moved to the cabinet in a corner where a large collection of automatic and semi-automatic weapons was stored.

After fifteen minutes had passed, the clank of meshing gears broke the silence as the aged and creaky elevator began its descent downward. A moment later, Aban Ashif was rolled to within a few feet of where Maddy stood. After eyeing the length of her, the old man turned to his aide and muttered something through yellowed and broken teeth that made Dorian smile lasciviously.

Gazing deeply at Ashif, Maddy was struck with the odd sensation that there was something familiar about him. Had they met before? Her thoughts were broken by the sound of Ashif's voice.

"It's not often that I have so beautiful a guest in my house," he said. "Welcome."

After introducing herself, Maddy got right to the point. "A friend of mine, Professor Liam Buchar, visited you recently," she said. "Since then, he's gone missing. It's critical that I find him. I'm hoping you can help me."

Ashif cocked his head and sat silently, as if trying to recall. As she awaited his reply, Maddy studied his face deeply, still trying to figure what was familiar about him.

Ashif finally spoke. "Sorry," he said, with a shake of his head, "But I don't recall anyone by that name." Ashif then turned in his chair to address his attendant. "Dorian," he said, tucking a strand of hair that had fallen into his face behind his right ear, "have we been visited by a Professor Buchar?"

With her eyes fixed on the old man's disfigured right ear, the realization hit Maddy like a thunderbolt. The familiar face, the deformed ear....

The man before her was Amber's father!

Chapter 38

On August 11th, Liam Buchar emerged from a dream to find everything warped, twisted and off-center. In his fantasy, he was drinking his fill of cold, clear water. Now, as he drifted back to consciousness, he became aware on an intense thirst raking the back of his throat. He had no idea of how long he'd been out, only that his mouth was taped shut with heavy material and his arms were pulled tight and tied behind his back. With a sluggish twist of his upper body, he yanked at the restraints that held him, only to trigger a painful pounding in his temples that made him groan. Straining to focus his eyes, he could make out nothing but empty blackness all around him. A minute or two later, the room began to swim out of focus and he sank back into a heavy slumber.

Over the next several hours, Buchar drifted in and out of consciousness. During one period of wakefulness, his eyes began to clear, and through heavy lids, he was able to survey his surroundings. He was at the end of a windowless room that, with the exception of a single bulb burning over a door in a far corner, was swallowed by darkness. The entire place - floor, ceiling, walls, even the door – was covered in heavy pile carpeting. On a far wall where the shadows were thick, he could make out a workbench and some tools on a rack, little sparks from the muted room light dancing off their shiny exteriors. To his right was a desk, where Buchar saw that his laptop had been placed. With the exception of a constant drone coming from an air conditioner overhead, the room was deathly quiet.

Sometime later, he was startled by the sound of a key turning in the door at the far end of the room. A moment later, the room's black void was sliced by a shard of light. With blood pounding in his temples, Buchar watched as a hand slithered around the half-open door, then saw a shadowed form lean in to stare at him before withdrawing. A minute later, he felt the narcotic pull him back to sleep. As the day wore on, he emerged from his stupor for increasingly lengthy periods, each time sensing that he was being observed by secret eyes. As his senses returned, he realized that his vision was beginning to clear and the pain in his head was gone, although his throat remained choked by thirst. Aware now of the hardness of the chair beneath him, he strained futilely to shift his weight.

Sometime later -- he had no way of knowing how long -- the door at the far end of the room swung open and Aban Ashif –guided by Dorian-- was rolled into the room. After positioning himself a few feet from where Buchar sat, Ashif, raising a bony finger, motioned to Dorian. The massive figure then stepped forward and with a yank, ripped the duct tape from Buchar's mouth, then untied the rope that had bound him.

With the smile on his face containing just a hint of mockery, Ashif spoke. "Good day professor, we've been waiting for you. We wanted you to awaken earlier, but Dorian here,"--at this point, Ashif nodded

in the direction of his companion--"overdid the dosage he gave you."
He shook his head ruefully. "It was very careless of him."

Buchar, grimacing from the pain in his throat, asked for some
water. Ashif signaled for Dorian to retrieve a bottle of water from a
refrigerator in the corner of the room. Taking the bottle, Buchar
poured half its contents down his throat. Then with water trailing
down his shirt, he fixed Ashif with a steely gaze.

"Ashif, you bastard," he spat, "why have you done this to me?"

"Me? I've done nothing. You are the cause of all this," he said,
edging his wheelchair so close to Buchar that Liam was assaulted by
the foul order coming from his decayed teeth. "When I told you
about the Seljuks and the First Order, I was merely playing with you,
as a cat might toy with mouse. I never dreamed you'd be able to find
out about the nineteenth-century Seljuks." He coughed up a small
laugh. "I have to give you credit professor," he continued.
"Deducing that we were using the Trithemius Cipher to encrypt the
Metrius virus was very clever."

"How did you find out?"

"You might be surprised," Ashif continued, "at the resources we
have at our disposal."

"You've infiltrated the U.S security agencies?" Buchar asked.
Ashif nodded.

"May I assume that your reach extends to the French security
agencies as well?"

Ashif smiled. Immediately, Buchar's mind flashed back to Phillip
D'Arnot and his snooping at the secure facility.

"Anyway," Ashif continued, "once we realized that you were making strides, we had to stop you. Unfortunately, we were too late. It appears that just before we got to you, you were successful in halting the destruction of the reactors."

Buchar, a sly grin spreading across his face, said nothing.

"And to make matters worse for us, we've accessed the files on your laptop. Apparently, you've encrypted your work with security measures that even our best minds can't crack." Ashif shook his head, an expression of regret marking his face. "A shame, really. Things were going so well." Ashif stared at Buchar through eyes that now resembled twin coals. "But now I'm afraid that we must insist that you reveal your password so we can reactivate the virus in time to meet our deadline," he said. "As you can see," he said, motioning to the desk against the wall, "we've brought your laptop to you."

"Of course," Buchar replied, "obtaining my cooperation may prove problematic."

"Not at all," Ashif replied casually. "You see, I have some very persuasive means at my disposal."

"Before we get to that," Buchar said, "there's something thing puzzles me."

"What's that?"

"Tell me, what the hell happened to you? You were always a little strange, but I never saw you as deranged. Now you intend to blackmail the world, destroy three great cities to get what you want?"

"First of all, my name is not Ashif. It's Deron Taham. I'm a

Palestinian nationalist and avowed enemy of Israel. Aban Ashif is a persona I established to gain entry into this country after I was reported killed in the 1987 uprising. I represented myself in academic circles as an expert on the Middle East. In that sense, I was being truthful. I am an expert. I'm also well-versed in the atrocities that have been committed against the Palestinian people. My life's work is to right a great injustice."

"And," Buchar replied, "kill millions of innocent people in the process?"

"As a great teacher once said, 'the ends justify my means,' If millions of infidel's should die, well," Ashif said with a shrug, 'it'll just be another day to me." Then, flipping his palms upward, he continued. "Which brings us to the present. You've managed to hide your work from us using security codes we can't crack. Unlock those codes so we can return the Metrius virus to an operational state."

Buchar snorted dismissively. "You're insane."

Ashif tilted his head in the direction of his servant. "Dorian can be pretty disagreeable," he said. "I'd encourage you to co-operate."

"Fuck you," came Buchar's reply. Then he turned toward Dorian. "And fuck your gorilla too."

Ashif shook his head. "How unfortunate," he said, Then turning to Dorian, he nodded. A moment later, Dorian approached Buchar and drove a fist into his face. The powerful blow shattered his front teeth and sent blood spraying into the air. For the next half-hour, the beating continued unabated, until fearful that Dorian might kill

Buchar, Ashif signaled him to stop. Then looming over the bloodied figure lying slumped on the floor, Ashif again asked if Buchar was ready to reveal the key to his security code. "Fu...fuck...you," came the halting reply from the wasted figure. Spouting a curse, Ashif signaled for Dorian to wheel him from the room.

For the next two days, the beatings took on a predictable pattern. In the morning, Dorian entered with Buchar's breakfast, generally consisting of two slices of dry toast and a pot of coffee. Sometime later, Ashif would be wheeled into the room, where he would remind Buchar of the date and time. The Fourth Order's deadline for destroying the plants was drawing near. It behooved Buchar, Ashif said, to reveal the key to his security codes. For if he didn't, they would surely kill him once the deadline had passed and the Fourth Order's threats were seen to be empty. After Buchar again refused to cooperate, Ashif would sigh heavily then motion to Dorian to resume his assault. By the morning of the third day of his capacity, Buchar's face was almost swollen beyond recognition and half of teeth had been loosened or completely knocked out.

With less than twenty-four hours to go before the plants were originally scheduled to explode, Ashif, at last realizing that Buchar would see himself killed rather than cooperate, grew agitated. "What do you want," he asked, his tone now desperate. "Money? I'll give you ten million dollars!" he said. "More money than you'll ever need. Just unlock your security codes so we can reactive the virus!" With disdain reflected in his eyes, Buchar stared at him through swollen eyes and made the reply with which Ashif had become so familiar. "Fuck you."

Pounding the arms of the chair in fury, Ashif spit out a string of epithets and instructed Dorian to wheel him away.

Chapter 39

Monday August 14th

After rejecting Ashif's offer of money, Liam Buchar fully expected his daily beatings to resume, but they did not. Instead, on August 14th , something happened that stunned him. It took place at 7:57 p.m Eastern time, just minutes before the Fourth Order's original deadline for destroying the plants was set to expire. Buchar was dozing in his chair when the door at the far end of the room flew open and Dorian appeared carrying a woman who appeared to be semi-conscious. Stepping to within a couple of feet where Buchar sat, Dorian dumped the body at his feet with a grunt.

It was Maddy Daniel.

A moment later, Dorian wheeled Ashif into the room.

"Good evening professor," he said smoothly. "We thought you would like a little company." Turning to Dorian, he instructed him to retrieve a chair and place Maddy a few feet from where Buchar stood. Once he did, he circled a rope just below her breasts to keep her from pitching forward, then secured her hands. As he did, Maddy, groaning heavily, slowly opened her eyes.

"Maddy," Buchar shouted, his eyes so wide that white was visible around his pupils, "Are you alright?"

Getting no response, Buchar turned toward his captor. "Ashif, you sick SOB, what have you done to her?"

"Just a slight knock on the head," Ashif replied, shifting his eyes to Maddy, who was now groaning audibly. "You see, she showed up yesterday, attempting to locate you." Ashif snickered. "It was very timely. She just might come in handy." Turning, he signaled for Dorian to retrieve a bottle of water from the refrigerator. Once he had, Ashif ordered him to splash water in Maddy's face. Maddy, with rivulets of water cascading down her face and breasts, started to squirm.

"What do you want with her?" Buchar demanded.

"Sadly, our methods of persuasion have proved inadequate at convincing you to cooperate with us. So now we're compelled to try something else." With that, Ashif nodded at Dorian. Reaching into his pocket, the attendant withdrew a pistol and moved to Maddy's side. Then cocking the weapon, he jammed it against Maddy's temple.

Ashif eyed Buchar. "Ok professor," he said, "the time for games is over. I'm going to count to three. Give us the key to your security code so we can meet our deadline or she dies."

"You bastard," Buchar spat, rising to advance on Ashif, only to have Dorian train the gun on him, freezing him in place.

"Not one more move, professor, or you're find yourself dead too."

Then fixing Buchar with a smug, crooked smile, Ashif began to count.

"One….."

Confronted with a conundrum that could only have arisen from the bowels of hell, Buchar recoiled. "Please!" he pleaded. "Please don't do this!"

"Two."

"I beg of you," Buchar screamed, his agitation reaching a fever pitch.

"Th----"

A cacophony suddenly broke from behind Dorian. With Buchar and Maddy watching in stunned amazement, Jason DeMir, armed with a pistol and fury showing in his face, bolted through the door, then after dodging a bullet from Dorian, proceeded to shoot Ashif dead on the spot. With Maddy and Liam ducking to avoid fire, Dorian took aim at Jason once more, this time, sending a bullet exploding into his right arm. Screaming in pain, Jason dived behind a chair for protection, then quickly switched the gun to his left hand and fired again. The first bullet missed its mark, but the second powered into Dorian's forehead and in a flash moment, brain matter and blood filled the air. Swaying for a moment, Dorian eyed Jason with an unfocused gaze, then with his eyes rolling back in his head, crashed dead to the floor.

Chapter 40

As Dorian collapsed, Buchar, recovering from the shock of what had just happened, moved to Jason's side.

"Are you alright?" Buchar asked.

Groaning and muttering, Jason gripped his arm and began to rock back and forth. With lurching steps, Buchar retrieved a towel and wrapped it around Jason's arm to staunch the bleeding. Next, he moved to Maddy's side and untied her.

With her head clearing, Maddy hugged Buchar, then turned to DeMir. "Thank God, Jason," she said. "We were about to be killed." DeMir flashed a weak smile.

"Professor," Maddy exclaimed, "we've got to get him to a doctor."

 Buchar, dashing toward his laptop, shook his head. "First I have to do something."

Maddy, wondering what could be more important that rushing Jason to a hospital, asked him what he was doing.

"I'm defusing the Metrius virus!"

"What!" Maddy exclaimed. "Didn't you already do that?"

 "Just the first operational phase," he said, flipping open his computer with a rapid motion.

"But Ashif thought---."

"That's what I wanted him to think.   But all I succeeded in doing was delaying the destruction of the plants."

"But how—"

Buchar, rushing his words, cut her off.

"I took a page from the Fourth Order's playbook," he said, frantically drumming his fingers on the desk, waiting for his computer to boot up. "Once I learned that Ashif was behind the plot, I used DNS poisoning to make my filesystems appear to be theirs. That enabled me to hack into their programs. But I only had time to delay the first operational phase which was scheduled for 8 p.m. before I was attacked."

"Disable or delay?" Maddy exclaimed, terror showing in her eyes.

"Delay," Buchar shot back. A moment later, his screen burst to life. "I was on the verge of completing the job when I was knocked out."

"Delay by how long?"

"Fifteen minutes," Buchar replied, his fingers flying over the keys of his laptop.

Maddy, shooting a glance at her watch, recoiled. "It's 8:11 pm on the east coast. Do you mean to say that all three plants will explode in three minutes?"

"That's exactly what I'm saying…. unless, I find a wi-fi hook-up right now!"

"Out here?" Maddy exclaimed. "There's nothing around for miles. Can't you use Ashif's connection?"

"Just tried," he said, shouting words over his shoulder. "It's password protected. But I spied a commercial development on my way up here. That's my best hope." At that moment, Jason groaned. Turning, Maddy saw that he'd pulled himself to a seated position.

"Any luck?" Maddy asked anxiously, turning back to Buchar.

"No! Time?"

Maddy, her eyes fixed on her watch, shouted a reply. "8:12!"

For the next forty seconds, Buchar furiously scanned the region for wi-fi connection. "8:13!" Maddy yelled.

"Got it!" Buchar exclaimed, stabbing the Enter key. "Now, gotta decrypt my files and upload the solution to the reactors."

Jason, roused by the atmosphere of crisis, struggled to his feet. "Is there a chance?"

Buchar, fingers flying over his keyboard, said nothing.

"8:14!"

"Got my files!" Buchar shouted. "Time?"

"Thirty seconds!"

"I might make it!" Buchar screamed.

Hearing a commotion coming from her left, Maddy, shot a glance at Jason. Stunned at what she saw, she dashed at DeMir with her arms flailing. A flash moment later, the gun in Jason's hand discharged sending a bullet deep into Buchar's brain.

Chapter 41

At the second that Liam Buchar's lifeless body hit the floor, the following message flashed on his computer screen:

Upload Complete.

He'd done it! With just seconds left, Buchar had saved the Metrius plants from destruction.

Switching her eyes from the message on Buchar's laptop, Maddy fixed her gaze on the exposed area of Jason's right arm.

"Long-sleeved shirts," she said, her eyes on the scar that was revealed by the torn shirt sleeve. "Even in summer," she said with a shake of her head, "always long-sleeved shirts. It's almost unbelievable."

"What?"

"The number of people you've managed to fool."

DeMir, his face an expressionless mask, eyed Maddy silently.

"Not to mention the number of people you've killed," Maddy continued. "Can I assume that I'm to be your latest victim?"

"I'm afraid so Maddy. With you out of the way, there's no one left to link me to any of this. Ashif will be ID'd as the evil figure behind the plot and I'll be free to continue my work." A darkening came over his face. "Anyway, even if it wasn't necessary to kill you, I probably would anyway. You see, you've made me very angry." He gestured at the lifeless figure of Liam Buchar on the floor, blood oozing from the wound on his head. "It was a beautiful plan. It took years to perfect and without his meddling and yours, it would've worked perfectly."

"Well, as long as you're going to kill me anyway, how about answering a question or two?"

DeMir shrugged.

"Why are you here? It's certainly not to save me."

"Finding you here was just a happy accident." Grimacing from the wound on his arm, he sat down with a groan. "You see, I was a protégé of Aban Ashif. I first encountered him years ago in the Syria as a child. When I was twelve, I, along with a group of fifteen other schoolboys, was abducted by a group of tribal extremists, with the promise that we'd be released after ten days. Of course, those days were filled with sessions on Islamic instruction led by Ashif himself. After ten days, he kept his word and we were allowed to return to our families. Or in my case, the distant relatives I'd been placed with after my family died. Most of the boys, though shaken by the experience, were otherwise unaffected. Not I. Everything I heard during those ten days made absolute sense. It was like I was seeing the world and the abuse that had been inflicted on Muslims for the first time. Days later, I said goodbye to my adopted family and returned to Ashif. That day, using a vial containing funeral ashes of Karil Fortos that Ashif had acquired years earlier, he marked me as a member of the Fourth Order. Once I was initiated, Ashif became the father that I never had."

"Some father figure," Maddy replied dryly. "A murderer and abuser of children."

"Say what you will," DeMir said, shifting in his chair, "but I'd had a terrible childhood to that point. And in me, Ashif saw the son he once had, but had lost. Once we were together, he showed me how to channel the anger and fear I felt over my upbringing into violence. It felt good. I was indebted to him."

"A debt you just repaid by watching him die."

He shrugged. "I guess people change," he said. "I recently learned that he was planning to betray me. You see, I was to be his heir and carry on his work. But I learned that he—" At this point, DeMir gestured to the crumpled form of Dorian lying on the carpet, "would be his successor, not me." He shifted his gaze to Maddy. "You can imagine my dismay." With his voice rising, he continued. "Remember that intruder at my apartment? That was no burglar, that was Dorian. Apparently he and Ashif decided I had to be eliminated. I knew then it was my life or theirs. So, here I am. Your being here was just a coincidence." He eyed the bodies strewn around the room. "So now, I will inherit the organization and carry on its work."

"And your friendship with Reid?"

"A complete and total set-up. The Order was familiar with the type of projects he was involved with. Big things, with a global reach. The kinds of projects we needed to further our goals. We monitored his social media accounts and knew in advance he'd be in Machu Picchu. Reid was always very open regarding his travels to South

America. The Order, using a bit of persuasion, got me a job tending bar at a place he frequented. In no time, he considered me to be his friend." DeMir smirked. "Can I help it if people find me charming?"

"But you saved his life!"

"What good was a dead techno wiz? For our plan to work, it was imperative for Reid to continue his work." He spat out a hearty laugh. "At least for awhile."

Maddy, who'd been staring at the floor as DeMir spun his tale of madness, lifted her head. "Tell me about the remote site in the desert, the charity and all the rest."

DeMir, a mocking tone in his voice, smiled. "You know, I get a kick out you Americans. Always complaining about the government and how it can't do anything right. Compared to the idiocy I see in the private sector, the government looks brilliant by comparison. Take Littleton Barry for example. Big shot CEO. Reputation for getting things done." DeMir snorted dismissively. "He was just another fool who bought into my charm. He was so busy running around accepting awards and shooting off his mouth, he had no choice but to delegate more and more responsibility to me. It reached a point where I could do anything I wanted with the Metrius Foundation. Working with Ashif, we cooked up the whole plot. First I siphoned off workers from Barry Incorporated and stuck them in the desert working on a source code project that was broken up into so many pieces, no one had a clue what was going on. The charity was part of it too. We needed a California site to set up the operational phases, the plans for which were communicated to our agents."

"How?"

"Using re-programmed smartphones."

"Why smartphones?"

"With the NSA and the U.S. security agencies monitoring everything, regular telephony and the Internet were just too risky."

"So Sahn Rameer, despite his ties to the charity, had nothing to do with this plot?"

"Nothing. Though we tried to get him to join us. One of our members, Farid Arsham, met with him in London in an effort to persuade him to return to his roots and work on behalf of The Order. But he was dedicated to the Metrius project and refused. After drugging our agent, he turned him over to Scotland Yard."

"And Amber's brother Marit?"

"Just a stupid Israeli agent," DeMir replied dismissively. "Though I admit he had us fooled for awhile. But over time we became suspicious. It was clear that we had a mole within our ranks. Knowing that he'd been detected, he left for California. It took awhile but we finally caught up him. One of our operatives slipped the polonium into his drink, then followed him back to his hotel and locked him in the suitcase." DeMir smiled at the thought. "A very creative way to package someone, we thought."

Maddy, disgusted at what she was hearing, shook her head. "And Rita Sessions?"

"Just a nobody who'd learned too much. We realized that she'd been in contact with Temple. We waited for him to leave that night and did what we had to."

"And Alison?"

"Same story. She was working with Rita. We'd tapped her phone and heard your conversation with her. The bomb that killed her? It was only partially successful. It was intended to kill all three of you."

"The three of us?"

"Yeah, the man who gave the bomb to Alison worked for Littleton and had no idea what was in the satchel. He was just an errand boy. But moments before giving the bag to Alison, Littleton called with something he had to do. It spared his life. And had you not stepped away before the bomb went off, we wouldn't be having this conversation now."

"All these murders. Life is pretty cheap to you and 'your order.'"

"The bodies could pile up like cord wood and still not match the dead on our side. Those who want nothing more than the freedom to practice their religion in the Middle East without interference from infidels."

"Do you really think you can get away with it? That the world would bow to your wishes?"

He shrugged. "This is just the first battle in a long war. A war that we will win."

"So," Maddy asked, fixing DeMir with a fiery gaze, "what have you got planned for me?"

"This."

DeMir lifted his gun, trained it on Maddy's abdomen and yanked the trigger. But instead of discharging, the hammer on DeMir's gun clinked harmlessly against the gun metal. DeMir, having used the last of his bullets to kill Buchar, was wielding a useless weapon.

In a flash, Maddy broke for the door, but DeMir was on her before she could escape. Struggling against him, she clawed at his eyes, frantically trying to break free. In desperation, Maddy tore into the deep wound on his right arm with her nails. Enraged, DeMir spat out a curse, then brutally smashed Maddy's face with his fist, knocking her to the floor.

Blood pouring from her mouth, Maddy lifted her head and through glazed eyes, saw DeMir turn his back to her, then heard him mutter something, his voice low and strange. An instant later, his body pitched forward, as if leaning into a strong wind. Maddy watched as his torso grew rigid, so rigid in fact that the pulsing of an artery in his neck became visible from where she lay. A moment later, she saw his arms fall away from his body and watched as he pulled himself up to his fullest height, his fists curled into balls of fury.

In a flash, Maddy realized that DeMir was psyching himself up, using thoughts to stoke his engine of madness as coal might stoke a steam engine. Then, when it seemed as if his rage might consume him, she saw him spin around and march toward her, hatred framed in his eyes. With gritted teeth and slits for eyes, he encircled her neck with his hands and bore down. Maddy, her life force depleted but not yet destroyed, flailed against him.

After a hellish minute, a gurgling sound bubbled up from Maddy's throat as her windpipe started to collapse. Her oxygen-starved brain began to shut down and she felt herself slipping away. Too depleted to fight back, Maddy let her body go limp, welcoming death and the peace that it would finally bring.

As her air-starved brain began to die, Maddy, in a dream now, felt herself being swept down a darkened corridor, twisting and tumbling past strange people with shadow faces, who were lined up shoulder-to-shoulder as if assembled to watch a passing parade. In a narrow space between two of the odd figures she spied Reid, dear Reid, watching with an odd detachment as she swept by. When she craned her neck to look back at him, she saw that he was pointing at something looming directly ahead of her. When she turned to see what it was, she realized she was being carried at great speed toward a yawning chasm whose edges loomed black and impenetrable, a wedge of broken light dancing at its center. As she drew closer to the opening, she felt herself suddenly infused with a serenity and awareness that she'd never experienced, as if energy emanating from the strange opening was dispersing a lifetime of blind unconsciousness.

Suddenly, from a faraway region, she sensed a discordant commotion. In a flash, she felt herself being pulled from the gateway she only moments earlier seemed destined to enter. She was aware now of shouting voices and strange movements, then heard a sharp explosion tear at a distant corner of her mind. In a flash, her throat - gulping, devouring, savoring - spasmed open, allowing a life-sustaining rush of cool air to burst into her lungs. As oxygen fed her brain, she was yanked back to the darkened room, fully aware now that Jason DeMir had crashed heavily to the floor beside her. Shooting a glance to her right, she saw Mako, in a marksman's stance, pistol raised and smoke still weaving from its barrel, mouthing the words 'You son of a bitch.' Standing behind her were Littleton Barry and Sahn Rameer.

Maddy attempted to call out, but her torn throat could produce no sound. As Littleton and Sahn checked to confirm that DeMir was dead, Mako rushed toward her friend with tears filling her luminous eyes. "Maddy! Are you all right?" she cried.

"Mako, what ...." Maddy's words were choked off by a coughing jag that doubled her over at the waist.

Mako anticipated her question. "How did we find you? Well, we have Farid Arsham to thank for that. Arsham had helped develop Metrius, but was also was working to sabotage the plants. Once in custody, Scotland Yard dangled a plea bargain in front of him that would shave years off his sentence. Arsham caved and spilled the entire story to the authorities."

Continuing to rub her throat, Maddy coughed. "But how did you find me?"

"Your friend Amber, knowing that you planned to visit someone named Ashif contacted GBS news trying to reach you. I ended up taking the call. She remembered that someone with that name was part of her father's cult. As it turned out, the real Aban Ashif had been killed years ago and following that, her father, seeking a new identity, took the name for himself. After talking to Amber, I contacted Littleton and Sahn, we added things up and well, here we are." Mako hoisted her pistol in the air and smiled triumphantly. "I knew all my target practice would come in handy one day!"

Mako, shifting her gaze to the lifeless form of Jason DeMir, shook her head. "Time for us to call the cops and have them collect this guy. It's the story of the century Maddy, and you'll be the one to break it."

Maddy said nothing. Her eyes may have been on Mako, but her thoughts were on a distant, windswept shore. In her mind's eye, she saw a sun-bleached day and an elegant, graceful man suspended in time and space, standing at the sea's edge. He stood peacefully and serenely, the pacing and anxiety that had once darkened his life ended now - melted into air, into thin air. And with the features of his handsome face flooded with brilliant sunlight, Maddy Daniel saw Reid Temple, with his vision for a better world finally realized, gazing joyfully into the horizon, completely and finally at peace.

www.ingramcontent.com/pod-product-compliance
Lightning Source LLC
Chambersburg PA
CBHW071147170626
46809CB00002B/806